Shane's voice dropped with a level of gravity she'd never heard before. "You have to listen to me."

Cassidy shook her head, steeling herself against the sight of her ex-husband. She couldn't stop herself from noticing he'd filled out over the past few years. Brown hair still spiked forward over his forehead, but the green eyes she'd first fallen for had darkened and grown wiser. His army combat uniform rode his shoulders in a way that spoke of lean muscle and sheathed strength.

This older version of Shane Logan carried himself like a man.

As always, the woman in her wanted to react to the man in him. Jerking her chin to the side, she called up her soldier facade. "Today's not the day for my ex-husband to step back into my life."

Something flashed in his eyes. "I understand that. And this isn't by choice." Shane took one short step into the room, but it was enough to back Cassidy tight against the wall. "You're not safe, Cassy."

He had no idea.

JODIE BAILEY

has been weaving stories since she learned how to hold a pencil. It was only recently she learned that everyone doesn't make up whole other lives for fun in their spare time. She is an army wife, a mom and a teacher who believes chocolate and a trip to the Outer Banks will cure all ills. In her spare time, she reads cookbooks, rides motorcycles and searches for the perfect cup of coffee. Jodie lives in North Carolina with her husband and her daughter.

FREEFALL

Jodie Bailey

Love Inspired

Recycling programs
for this product may
not exist in your area.

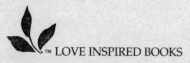 ™ LOVE INSPIRED BOOKS

ISBN-13: 978-0-373-67536-4

FREEFALL

Printed in U.S.A.

Love does not delight in evil but rejoices
with the truth. It always protects, always trusts,
always hopes, always perseveres.
                    —*1 Corinthians* 13:6–7

To Paul: You really are everything I never knew I needed. God knew it would take you to make me totally me. He's awesome like that. I love you.

And to Cailin: I love you infinity times infinity. Plus one.

ONE

The explosion blasted a tidal wave of sound through the yellow cinder block walls, rocking the building like an earthquake.

Army Chief Warrant Officer Cassidy Matthews's hands flew to the back of her head. She dived for cover on the floor, cracking her forehead against the top of the desk. Her sinuses rattled. Stars shot through her vision. For an instant, the room evaporated, and the foul oiliness that permeated the air of Iraq overwhelmed her.

Only this wasn't Baghdad.

"Mac!" She shook her head to clear her vision and inventoried the room. No blast holes in the wall. Roof intact. No smoke. But where was Master Sergeant McIntyre? He'd been standing right in front of her not ten seconds earlier. Planting her hands on her desk, Cassidy pushed herself to her feet just as Mac braced his hands opposite hers and rose to meet her eyes.

Mac's eyes scanned the room. "You okay, Chief?"

With a quick nod, Cassidy ducked around the older man and headed for the windows that overlooked the enormous wooden tables on the parachute packing floor below. The few riggers who were packing their quota of static line chutes before lunch raced for the door, their muffled shouts a strong indicator that whatever went off was right outside the large concrete and cinder block Eighty-Second Airborne Rigger Shed.

She whirled to Mac. "Get down there. Stop them from exiting the building before we know what's going on. The last thing we need is—"

"To draw fire if this is some kind of setup?"

Cassidy's exhale almost echoed off the walls of her office. Not on Fort Bragg. Surely they were safe here. "Corral them the best you can."

Sergeant Erin Landon appeared in the doorway, wisps of her wavy brown hair straggling from the knot beneath her red rigger's cap. Sweat sheened her forehead, which creased her porcelain skin into deep lines over dark blue eyes. "Chief, Private Anderson's car just went up in the parking lot."

With a glance back, Mac disappeared out the door.

"Anderson's car? Where is Anderson? Right now?" *Please don't say he's in his car.* Cassidy snatched the phone and dialed 9-1-1, the receiver quaking in her hand. "Find him. Make sure he's—" The words refused to come. Anderson was a green private, new to the company as of a couple of months ago, fresh out of basic and rigger school. He couldn't be more than nineteen.

She had to know all of her soldiers were okay. "Never mind." As the operator answered, she thrust the phone at Landon. "Tell them what's going on." Without waiting to see if the sergeant followed her order, she brushed past her, racing for the stairs.

Lungs burning and heart thumping so hard he could hear it, Major Shane Logan pushed harder and tried to keep a line of sight on the man he pursued across the parking lot. It got harder by the second. The advantage tipped the wrong way. The July heat worked against him in his desert boots and Army Combat Uniform. The man ahead of him wore jeans and running shoes. Every thud of foot on pavement reinforced the difference.

The pair plunged into a maze of shipping containers on the back side of the parking lot. By the time Shane skidded around the corner of the second trailer-sized container, the man had disappeared. His eyes roamed the sea of identical tractor trailer-sized containers and stopped. The guy could be anywhere.

Sweat burned his eyes. How did he get here anyway? If this day had gone as planned, by now he'd have a soda in his hand, baseball on the TV and two weeks of vacation stretching before him. He should have minded his own business. Instead, he had to come and see for himself whether or not what his interpreter in Afghanistan had told him was true. Someone was using the parachutes returning from the war zone to smuggle Afghan opium into the country.

The smart move would have been to let the authorities handle it, but no. He'd shown up in time to spot someone bolt from a souped-up Honda near the building just before it exploded in a shower of flame.

The container door twanged a hollow rattle as he slapped his palm against it. Shane gave up the chase and dropped against white-hot metal. He propped his hands on his knees, gulping thick air that didn't do anything to slow his heart rate.

Shouts and sirens overtook the pounding in his ears as his body settled down. Pressing his hands against the container, he pushed himself upright and trudged toward his truck.

The torched Honda lofted oily smoke into the air. Yellow fire trucks rounded the corner with sirens squealing and pulled into the parking lot, firemen at the ready.

Shane reached his truck and snatched his cell phone off the seat in disgust. No power. The battery in the thing died on a whim if it wasn't plugged in nightly. Fat lot of help it was right now.

He let his eyes drift toward the fire as he pocketed the device. Through the smoke, soldiers gathered on the far side of the parking lot. One stood apart from the others, shoulders slumped until he almost bent double. Probably his car. Poor kid. No telling how much of his enlistment bonus he'd dropped on jazzing that thing up.

Shane leaned his hip against the side of the truck and crossed his arms, waiting for the Military Police to arrive so he could describe what he'd seen. Because all he'd gotten a good look at was a black T-shirt and jeans, he doubted anything he said would do much good. At least he could convince them this most likely wasn't an accident.

Movement at the near end of the loading dock caught his eye. A side door opened, and two other soldiers—a middle-aged man and a tall, slim blonde—stepped out. They stopped to view the carnage, and she appeared to give orders before he walked off and she turned in Shane's direction.

His heart, which had returned to normal after his full-tilt flight across the parking lot, thudded to his feet. He straightened and squinted against the sunlight. It couldn't be her. It just…couldn't be.

Before he could duck and cover, she pivoted on one heel and stalked across the loading dock in the direction of the soldiers on the other side of the lot.

Releasing the breath he hadn't realized he held, Shane sidestepped toward the bed of his truck to keep her in view. It was her all right. In almost a decade, her stride hadn't changed.

Scattered thoughts clicked like tumblers in a lock.

It appeared she was in charge of the rigger shed. Everything his contact had told him pointed to…

Cold sweat broke out along his back. It all indicated his ex-wife was the target.

"Nitrous? Over the fuel line?" Genius. Cassidy wanted to pound her palm against her forehead. The amount of money some of these guys poured into their cars—either to look cool or to boost the engines for street races—could buy her an early retirement and a house on the coast. She stopped herself before she rolled her eyes heavenward.

Private Anderson's chin dipped, and his shoulders tipped forward before he caught himself and straightened. He was wound so tight even his close-cropped red hair seemed to shiver.

"Is that even legal, because I'm pretty sure it's not *street* legal?" Cassidy looked over the private's shoulder at Master Sergeant McIntyre, who shrugged and shook his head. She turned her attention to the younger man. "You hooked nitrous to your car last night. In the barracks parking lot, under the supervision of your buddies who have zero experience in the process. Am I tracking? Have I got it straight?"

"We didn't actually leave it hooked up, ma'am. I think that's the illegal part." Anderson stared at a spot just over her shoulder. "Ma'am."

Oh, how she wanted to confine this kid to quarters for walking the line just this side of stupid. But it wasn't her place to dish out that kind of discipline and, try as she might, she couldn't find one single thing he'd actually done wrong. "I really, really hope you had your car insured."

At the hint of his charred vehicle, the private's expression slipped even further. "I did," he muttered.

"Doubt they'll cover after-market parts like nitrous, though."

"I don't think the nitrous…" He shook his head. "I'll check, ma'am."

Cassidy bit the inside of her lip. It was already well past the end of the duty day, a day in which the investigation ate up their time and put them behind on the number of parachutes packed for the Eighty-Second Airborne Division's soldiers. The chute riggers would have been finished and gone already if the fireworks in the parking lot hadn't locked them all down until the investigators found the source of ignition. "Go ahead. You're dismissed. And you're lucky this little stunt didn't get your buddies all stuck here for the whole weekend. It's a post-9/11 world. Nobody likes it when things go boom on a military base." She waved a hand toward the door. "Keep me posted on what happens, and I have a pretty strong hunch the commander will want to meet with you sooner rather than later when he gets back."

Snapping a salute, Anderson was out the door,

through the outer office, and already on the stairs before Cassidy could blink.

She looked from the door to McIntyre as she sank against the front of her desk. "Think he's scared?"

"More like grief-stricken. His baby just went bye-bye. A guy like Anderson would sooner break up with a hot girlfriend than get a scratch on his car. Imagine what this kind of carnage is doing to his soul." He leaned against the door frame and crossed his arms over the rank on his chest. "He'll get over it eventually. Think about it. The kid just bought himself legend status in the Division. He'll forever be the guy whose car went up like the Fourth of July in the parking lot of the rigger shed. They'll still talk about him when they're in their seventies and swappin' stories at the VFW hall."

Straightening, Cassidy took the three steps across the room to the windows that looked down at the cavernous parachute packing area below, where Anderson huddled with several of his buddies by one of the long wooden pack tables. "You really think he'll be okay?" Try as she might, she couldn't always stop the mothering instinct as it surged in her.

"Yeah. I imagine as long as he didn't have the bottle hooked up, insurance will cover most of it. He'll get something new and shiny, and he'll have a reputation to boot. He's one bad dude now."

She snickered and glanced over her shoulder at him. "Know what? I think it's time we both got out of here. The fire's out, Criminal Investigation Division is done and has released us to go. There's no reason to stick around. Sergeant Jamison and Private Reynolds are locking up tonight. If you herd the rest of the crew out, you can get home to your wife."

Mac straightened. "Works for me. See you Monday?"

"Yeah. Hopefully nothing will go up in smoke between now and then." She waved as Mac rounded the corner into the main office, then turned her attention to the floor below. Normally, the warehouselike room was filled with riggers carefully inspecting and meticulously packing the parachutes that kept the "airborne" in the Eighty-Second Airborne Division. Now, after the excitement of this day, only a small knot stood between the tables and the door. From the looks of the small group, they'd ended the consolation portion of their day and had moved on to ribbing Anderson about his car. Circle of life or something like that.

Cassidy rested her forehead against the glass and studied them. In some ways, it felt like only a few weeks since she'd been a red-hatted rigger herself. Today, she felt every one of the days between then and now, days when she'd fought through quartermaster school, battled her private demons and emerged as one of the few females to ever sit in her position as Division Parachute Officer. Most days, it was an accomplishment that squared her shoulders and lifted her chin. Right now, the weight of her responsibility anchored her to the spot, too heavy to let her move.

"You and I both know nitrous isn't flammable." The voice over her shoulder yanked a gasp from her throat as her spine whipped straight.

Familiarity froze her feet to the floor before she could whip around. Not that voice. Not today. She'd spent years trying to let it go, to stop dreaming about it when she slept. The warm chills that washed over her in a haze of long-forgotten memories was almost as unwelcome as the blast that had corkscrewed this day sideways hours before.

Those were memories Cassidy should have released long ago and which should certainly not be drawing her in now. She gripped the ledge of the window so hard that her fingers burned against the painted cinder block. "When I turn around in three seconds, you'd better be a figment of my imagination."

"I'd make that happen for you if I could, but today's not the day. Cassy," the voice dropped with a level of gravity she'd never heard before, "you have to listen to me."

She shook her head, steeled herself against the sight of him and let go of the wall, her only anchor in a world rocking sickeningly out of control. The minute she turned, Cassidy wished she'd kept her grip. She couldn't stop herself from noticing he'd filled out over the past few years. Brown hair still spiked forward over his forehead, but the green eyes she'd first fallen for had darkened and grown wiser. His Army Combat Uniform rode his shoulders in a way that spoke of lean muscle and sheathed strength. His jaw was squarer, his demeanor more confident. This older version of Shane Logan carried himself like a man, not an immature little boy playing dress up in a soldier's body.

As always, the woman in her wanted to react to the man in him. It would take effort, but she'd choke that desire out in short order. Jerking her chin to the side, she called up her soldier facade. "And today's not the day for my ex-husband to step back into my life." She drew in a deep breath and tried to still the quake in her voice. "I'm pretty sure that's a day that's never going to come."

A quick flash of something in his eyes was the one indication he gave that the bullet met its mark before he pulled himself a spare inch taller. "I understand that. And this isn't by choice." Shane took one short step into the room, but it was enough to back Cassidy so tight against the wall that she felt the window ledge press against her bones. "You're not safe, Cassy."

He had no idea. It took a strength she hadn't had to rely on since her last combat tour, but she shoved aside the emotions his sudden appearance dragged up. On a normal day it would take too much energy to do battle with him. Today, too many reminders of war zone improvised explosives had stolen every ounce of her reserves. "Not as long as I've got cars blowing up in my parking lot and an ex who ought to be long gone sneaking up on me. I told you, Shane. Not today. Walk out, let another decade go by, and maybe I'll feel more like listening to what you have to say." With no little effort, she brushed past him and strode to her desk, where she shuffled papers in an obvious effort to ignore him. "You found your way in, you can find your way out."

The quick thud of his boots didn't give her enough warning. His fingers clasped her biceps and pulled her back around to face him before the sound fully registered against her ears. His gaze pinned hers with a force his grip couldn't match. "Someone is trying to kill you."

Cassidy jerked away, fighting the urge to step around her desk in an effort to use it as a barrier between them. Instead, she went against every instinct and stood taller, her nose inches from his. "Then they torched the wrong car." Planting her palm against his chest, she shoved him out of her personal space, space he hadn't invaded in years. "Did you come back from your last mission with posttraumatic stress riding your back?" Then again, the way her pulse was reacting to him right now, she was likely the one with stress issues. Why was she even letting him stand here? After what he'd done…

Anger flared at herself for letting him goad her senses. "Know what? Just go." Cassidy rounded her desk, ashamed at herself for hiding. "I've had more than enough—"

"You're missing a shipping container."

The declaration choked off the rest of her words. "Wh—" Cassidy's knees lost their strength, threatening to drop her hard into her chair. She knuckled the top of her desk. This was information she'd only just received that morning. "How did you know that?"

"It's not important." Shane flattened his palms against the top of her desk and leaned toward her. "Someone on the other side is packing your parachutes with heroin and shipping it back to the States."

Cassidy stood and held her hands up between them to put a stop to this crazy train. Shane was clearly out of his head. "I don't know how you found out about the missing CONEX, but that last part? You've lost your mind. You can't come in here on a day like today and start messing with my head." Her fingers wrapped around the receiver of her desk phone. "You've got ten seconds to get out before I call the MPs back here to have them talk to you."

For a full half minute, Shane eyed her as though he were trying to judge the veracity of her threat, then his shoulders lost some of their squareness in acceptance. "Fine. For now."

"No. For good." Cassidy rounded the desk, careful not to brush her sleeve against Shane's shoulder, and marched toward the door. "Ten years hasn't been long enough for me to be ready to listen to you again."

Before Shane could respond, motion from the outer office jerked Cassidy's attention sideways.

Jackson Reese straightened from where he'd been leaning against the edge of the counter on the far side of the room, his brow creased. "Everything okay, Cass?"

Cassidy glanced from her friend to Sergeant Erin Landon, who stood a few feet from Jackson, arms crossed, studying her right back. "It's fine. Major Logan was just leaving."

Ignoring Shane's attempt to catch her eye, she focused her attention on Sergeant Landon as he brushed past her and disappeared at the door to the stairs. As soon as he was gone and the pressure in her chest eased, she spoke to the younger woman. "Did you need something, Sergeant?"

"I—" She took a step away from Jackson and shook her head. "You looked so upset earlier, ma'am. I wanted to come up before I left and make sure you were okay."

"I am." Cassidy never had been able to read Landon. Since the day the girl had arrived last winter, it had been hard to tell if her gestures were genuine or edged with sarcasm. If this wasn't the army, she'd swear that woman was angling for her job. "You can go."

As the younger woman's bootfalls echoed in the stairwell, Cassidy turned to Jackson and caught him watching the door. "You know her?" She turned and headed back into her office, certain he'd follow.

"Her? Nope. Cute, though, isn't she?"

"If you like the thick wavy hair, pale skin, super-model type." Cassidy shook her head and dropped into one of the chairs in front of her desk. "Still not quite sure how a girl like her survived basic. She's so…"

"Not a soldier?" Jackson rounded her desk and dropped into her chair, leaning forward and clasping his hands together over her paperwork.

"You could say that. She definitely toes the line when it comes to overstepping her position. Landon makes me feel like she's just letting me think I'm the one in charge."

"And yet there's nothing you can specifically bust her on, right?" He eyed her until she nodded. "So, who was the major you were in here with? You need me to go after him and tell him it's not a good idea to visit with you again?" Ever since he'd taken care of a couple of contractors in Afghanistan who thought she might like to be their plaything, he viewed himself as her protector. Typically, the role didn't bother her, but when it came to Shane…

"No. And I doubt you will see him again anyway." Shane had waited forever to make this reappearance in her life, so why had he picked today? Weary with the day, weary with Shane's intrusion and weary with life in general, Cassidy dug for a sense of normalcy that would take away the dull throb in her head. "So, who told you I could use a friendly face?"

Jackson relaxed and ran his hand through thick blond hair. "Word travels fast. Heard you had a little excitement over here and thought I'd come over and check on you." His brown eyes grew dark with concern. "You okay?"

"Other than thinking I was back in Baghdad for a few minutes, I'm fine." *I'd be even better if the past hadn't picked today to intrude.*

"Yeah, I'd imagine that kind of noise would trigger a flashback or two." He aimed a finger at her forehead. "How did you get the bruise?" Anger flashed in his eyes, and he straightened. "It wasn't that guy, was it?"

"What? No, not at all." Shane had never laid a finger on her, nor had she ever feared he would. If anything, he was overly protective. Cassidy pressed her fingertips to a spot above her right eyebrow and winced at the sting. "Desk diving." She grabbed her laptop and shoved it into the case as she glanced at her desk for her ID card. "At least it wasn't a car bomb. More like mechanical ineptitude."

"So they know what caused it?"

Cassidy nodded, relieved to talk about anything but Shane, even if it was an exploding vehicle.

Jackson relaxed and leaned back in her chair. "A little too much power in those modifications, huh?"

"Boys and their toys." She shrugged and glanced at her computer, wanting nothing more than to mark this day down as a distant memory. "Hey, see if you see my ID card anywhere."

Easing the chair back, Jackson eyed the floor beneath her desk. "You lost it?"

"Actually, I'm not sure. I had just pulled it out of the card reader on my computer when the explosion happened. I must have launched it somewhere."

Jackson laughed, but it was different from his usual, easy laugh.

Cassidy looked at him, but he was doubled over, searching under her desk. With a shake of her head, she wrote the cold tingle in her spine off to post-explosion adrenaline and Shane-induced emotions. "Not funny, my friend. You try thinking you're under attack on home soil sometime."

"Been there, done that, liking my cushy contractor job over at Brigade now, thank you very much. So far, nothing's blown up outside my building."

"You're lucky I like you." She scanned the baseboards behind her desk.

"Got it."

Cassidy looked up to find Jackson holding her ID card between two fingers. "It was under your desk."

"That's a relief. It would be an international incident if I lost that thing."

"Ah, it's not that bad. It'd just raise the domestic terror threat level to red for a couple of hours." Jackson winked as he straightened and ran his hand down his polo over his chest. "Want to grab some dinner? You can tell me all about your visions of chaos, and I can tell you all about how Lauren dumped me last night."

This time Cassidy winced. "Ouch. She did?"

He cocked his arm and swung like he was taking a major league pitch. "Strike three. I'm out. Reese takes the walk of defeat back to the dugout."

"Yeah, okay." She ushered him out of the room and flipped off the light, then pulled the door shut behind her. "If I know you, there are six more in the bullpen waiting to pitch to you."

"You one of 'em?"

Her laugh was hollow as she tested the door lock. What made him bring that up today? Of all people, Jackson knew best that she would never be involved in another relationship, not without some sort of lifetime guarantee. Something that said if it broke, she could get her wasted years back. "You know better. I'll let you take me to dinner. Then I'm going home to start my weekend. My nice, *quiet* weekend."

Breaking and entering. That's what this amounted to, even if the guy who got to the house before him and was still in there had been the one to pick the lock for the actual "breaking." And because it was Cassy's house, it might amount to his ceasing to draw breath if she found him here. She'd made it more than clear she wasn't happy to see him earlier.

Shane slipped the back door closed and stopped. Thunder rumbled in the distance, and the late-evening light outside faded. He stared across the kitchen, listening for sounds of movement in the house.

He'd left her office determined to make her see the danger she faced. If she refused to believe the truth and something happened to her that he could have prevented...

It hadn't taken much effort to find out where she lived, but his intention to wait in the driveway and try to talk to her was thwarted when he drew near the house and saw the man he'd chased earlier slip into the side door of the garage. His only thought had been to protect Cassy, so he'd parked down the street and edged along the side of the travel trailer sitting on the lawn to the left of the garage, noting it still bore the bumper sticker from when Cassy and he had taken it on their first trip to the Outer Banks of North Carolina.

A rustling above his head stilled his movements. For an instant, he thought about charging up the stairs to play hero, but he had no idea of the lay-out of the house. If the intruder heard him coming and hid, he wouldn't have a prayer of getting out of this without a confrontation he'd have to explain to the police. Shane couldn't see that one ending well. They'd forget all about the arsonist he'd followed and want to know what he was doing uninvited inside his ex-wife's house. *Know what the penalty is in North Carolina for stalking, son?*

There had to be a way to draw the guy out, get eyes on him. Shane let his gaze travel the room again as a soft thud drifted through the ceiling. And there was his answer, lying on the counter in front of the toaster oven. A garage door opener.

Shane crept along the granite counter, snagged the opener and slid into the short hallway between the kitchen and what appeared to be a dining room. Pressing his back against the wall, he pushed the button and shifted into a defensive position as the garage door's movements rumbled through the walls.

A curse and a flurry of noise echoed from above, then silence engulfed the house.

Trying to discern slight sounds, Shane held his breath. No footsteps thudded toward him. Surely he wasn't headed for the front door. Maybe...

Adrenaline jerked at his muscles. Was the guy lying in wait for Cassy? Shane narrowed his eyes and hit the button again, listening as the door ground into place, ready to defend if necessary. If it was Cassy they wanted, it was Cassy they'd think they were getting.

Easing around the corner, Shane opened what he judged to be the garage door and slammed it, then slipped back to his hiding place.

A man stood in front of him, silhouetted by the dining-room windows. Muted light glinted off the blade of a knife.

Shane judged the other man's bulk in an instant. His adversary had two inches and twenty pounds on him. That, and there was the blade of the knife that made height and weight irrelevant.

Well, nobody had ever said going against a drug smuggler would be easy. Ducking his head, Shane lowered his shoulder and charged.

TWO

"You have got to be kidding me." Cassidy dropped her head against the back of her SUV's seat and stared through the Trailblazer's windshield into thick, gooey darkness. It was like Murphy and his laws followed her around, blowing up cars in the parking lot, inviting her ex-husband into her office, knocking her power out in a storm just as her garage door closed.

There wasn't a tornado warning she didn't know about, was there? Because it sure wouldn't surprise her if she blinked and found herself in a storm-tossed Kansas cornfield.

Maybe she'd forget the idea of her bed and sleep right here. The way things were going, her cell would ring and the soldier on twenty-four-hour staff duty would call her back into work anyway.

Thunder cracked a shudder through her. It was doubtful she'd ever get over the adrenaline rush that came with booming thunderstorms, especially if cars insisted on blowing up outside her office.

The army had been easier when she was younger. Multiple trips to the "Sandbox" of Iraq and the mountains of Afghanistan had sapped her of any form of resilience. That and, apparently, thirty-four was the age when bounce-back time doubled. Her own bed and a sound sleep couldn't come soon enough. Maybe when she woke up, it would be easier to pretend this entire day had been a nightmare.

Even her metal flashlight felt heavier than usual as she grabbed it from under the seat and opened the car door. It wouldn't do to survive a war zone only to break her neck tripping over a rake in her own garage.

Reaching across the console, she snatched the paper bag that held her supper. Halfway to their cars, Jackson had received a phone call that forced him to cancel, so Cassidy stopped and picked up a thick, juicy burger at the corner grill near the house. Her stomach urged her to drop to the concrete and inhale the thing right there, but eating in the dark made her nervous, especially after the time she'd spent with all sorts of creepy-crawly critters on the other side of the world. Scorpions and camel spiders would probably always haunt her nightmares. The way they skittered... She shuddered again and gingerly set one foot on the ground, half expecting something to wriggle up her shin.

She inched her way to the kitchen door. Once she made it safely inside with her neck intact, Cassidy killed the flashlight and flipped the mudroom light switch.

Of course. Nothing. A quick glance across the kitchen through the back windows told her she wasn't the only one who'd be suffering part of this summer night without air-conditioning. She groaned. And it was raining. There wouldn't be any open windows to relieve the heat. Wonderful.

Cassidy tipped her neck to the side and stretched tight muscles. She still reveled in the spicy smells and warm comfort of her own house after her deployments overseas. Central air and hot showers and overhead lighting were things she'd never take for granted again. Well, she wouldn't once the power came back on anyway.

A strange sixth sense sent little spider footsteps down her spine and raised cold chills in their wake. Something wasn't quite right. Must be the darkness. More light. She needed more light. There were candles on the coat closet shelf. She flipped on her flashlight and yanked open the closet door.

Eyes gleamed back at her.

As she stepped back, the paper bag holding her hamburger slipped through her fingers and thudded to the floor. A scream refused to work its way from her lungs to her throat. It stuck somewhere in the middle and blocked her ability to breathe. Before her body could react, a shadowed figure pushed her against the door, body heavy against hers as a hand pressed against her mouth. The flashlight clattered against the linoleum and rolled away.

"Don't scream." The hiss grated against her ears.

She struggled and fought the weight that pressed against her. No way was she going out like this, not after all she'd been through. If it was her time to die, she'd make sure her attacker bore marks he wore to his grave. Her body went limp, then she raised her knee, grateful for heavy combat boots and praying to connect with a foot when she forced her heel toward the floor. Her boot made contact with a satisfying *thud,* and her attacker's grip loosened and fell away. Cassidy crouched and prepared to launch.

"Cassy, don't charge. I'm not going to hurt you." The words came from the menacing shadow directly in front of her.

Cassidy stumbled, and the coiled spring inside of her unwound with a snap as words penetrated her adrenaline-driven thoughts. For the second time in one day, that never-forgotten voice invaded her conscious. Her fists clinched tight. Shane didn't deserve any less of a beating than a random, violent invader. A flash of lightning burned the shape of him into her eyes as she renewed her attack position. "You've got three seconds to get out of my house, Shane. I have no idea what makes you think this is okay."

"I wasn't sure it was you coming in, so I hid the first place I could find." His measured voice moved to the right. "Listen to me. Somebody's been in—"

"You have got to be kidding me. Isn't it enough you showed up spouting crazy stories at my job on the most chaotic day ever? Get out." There was no way she'd listen to anything he had to say. She spotted the beam of her flashlight shining at a crazy angle onto the refrigerator. Every good soldier knew a Maglite had enough heft to be an effective weapon, and it might feel good to swing it if she had to. She snatched it and held it high, prepared to strike. "I will use this on you, and I will call the cops and I will tell them it was self-defense."

"This is important."

"I've got no reason to listen to you. Know why? Because the years haven't been long enough to make me forgive you. You're not my husband. You're not part of my life. You don't even exist, as far as I'm concerned. We're not rehashing this." The beam of the flashlight arced higher as Cassidy cocked her swinging arm. "Now go." Her heart beat so hard it pulsed in her eyeballs. It could be fear, anger or...

She shook her head. No. It was fear or anger. Nothing more.

"I know who I used to be. I did a lot of things wrong, but you've got to—"

Cassidy's head tilted back, her jaw jutting between them as if it could block the emotions that struggled to surface. "Don't try to explain yourself."

"Fine." Shane sounded like each breath was an effort, and she could just make out the hulk of his dark shape between her and the kitchen. "I heard a rumor on my last mission, and when I went to check it out—"

"Spare me. Special Forces changed you, and I don't care about your last mission or any of your other missions. It was bad enough to never know when you were leaving or where you were, but not knowing who you were after you got back? Watching you stumble home after drinking all night with your buddies?" She jerked the flashlight. "Hearing you—"

Rapid pounding blasted against the front door.

Cassidy's heart leaped out of her chest and she fought to inhale against the memories and the present, then a familiar voice called her name. It sliced through her fear and robbed her muscles of their readiness.

Her gaze shifted from Shane to the kitchen, and she hissed, "You're out the door. Now. Discussion closed. I can't do this with you."

"Who's that?"

Shane's jealousy-laden voice made Cassidy straighten her shoulders. "Jackson. Maybe you saw him at my office? He's a contractor who worked on the forward operating base during my last deployment. *He's* trustworthy." She backed two steps across the kitchen. "And he'll tear the door down if he thinks something's happened to me." She tipped the flashlight beam in Shane's direction, not one bit guilty about omitting the fact that Jackson was a good friend and nothing more. Shane could suffer with his assumptions…if he suffered at all.

Her heart missed a step when the light hit his face. It was a reaction her emotions weren't ready for in spite of the fact he'd stood before her earlier. The intervening years had dulled his image in her mind, and the flash of his features in the light shot long-forgotten memories across her heart.

The pounding on the door grew more insistent, and she glanced over her shoulder, torn between the man she used to love and her would-be protector.

"You and I are both in danger. Until I know more, nobody can know I'm here. Please, Cassy." His voice pleaded as his shadowed form slipped into the closet.

Cassidy stared at the door. In danger? The only danger she could see in her house right now was him. Her fingers gripped the doorknob as Jackson called for her again. She wavered, then decided Jackson would either burst in or call for reinforcements if she didn't respond soon. She jogged toward the living room, unable to determine if anything about this bizarre evening warranted a phone call to the police.

Shane pressed his ear to the closet door and fought the urge to grip his biceps. It throbbed after the exertion of subduing Cassidy. He'd forgotten how strong she was. Worse, he'd forgotten how she felt in his arms. It had taken only a moment of contact to drive the images through his memory like they'd just been together yesterday.

He shook his head. Now was the worst time for a long drive through their distant past. If he fell into old habits with her, there'd be no way to ensure she had a future. And considering he'd fended off a knife-wielding stranger in her house tonight, both of their futures might be shorter than either of them could imagine.

Only muffled, indistinguishable voices reached his ears, so he gave up eavesdropping and dropped his forehead against the door. His eyes narrowed. Who was this "trustworthy" Jackson who felt so protective of Cassy? And, for that matter, why did he care? They'd both barricaded that door a long time ago. He didn't love her. Wouldn't love her. Even though touching her just now had flooded his senses with vivid reminders of touching her in the past.

He pressed his fists into the door and shook his head. When he'd married her fourteen years ago, he'd promised to protect her. Yeah, the relationship ended in front of a judge four years later, but he wasn't the kind of man to let a promise of that magnitude die. Whether Cassy knew it or not, she needed protecting now more than ever. He should go out there right now...

His fingers unclenched. If he blew his hiding place out of some misplaced jealousy, there might not be another shot at discovering who was out to hurt her. It was just that, for all he knew, this Jackson joker had his hands all over what was going down in Cassy's unit.

Yeah, right. That would be a hundred-yard stretch. Jackson was probably some smarmy little horn-rimmed glasses accountant type with a bald spot and allergies that would—

Footsteps, heavy ones, thumped toward him. It took a second, but he recognized the cadence of Cassy's stride in her boots. Surely she wasn't mad enough to throw open the door and reveal him after he'd asked her not to. He squeezed his eyes shut, body tense, and prayed. Shane had seen the face of the man who blew up that car and broke into Cassy's house. Now she wasn't the only one in danger. He was in this with both feet and sinking fast.

The steps passed, and a door creaked open. There was silence, then the same door closed again.

"Got it." Cassy's voice floated into the closet and sent a familiar tremor down his spine. "Good thing I left it in my truck or I might have dropped it when… when I tripped coming into the house." Her footsteps slowed as she neared the closet.

Shane pressed his forehead tighter to the door, his hands flat-palming the cool wood. She was so close he could almost feel her.

She picked up speed and passed.

He'd always known he'd see her again someday. The army was too small, their jobs too specialized, to avoid certain confrontation. But of all the ways he'd imagined a reunion, this wasn't one of them. Sure, he'd known all along it wouldn't be roses and kittens, but he never figured he'd be hiding in her coat closet bleeding from a stab wound in his arm.

And he'd never imagined he'd feel anything other than coldness for the woman who'd thrown their marriage to the pavement and ground it under her boot heel. Shane leaned his head against the door. *God, help me. I can't fall in love with her again.*

Cassidy dropped to the sofa and bent to untie her bootlaces, doing her best to act normal while her mind searched for topics that had nothing to do with explosions or Shane. He could stay in her closet all night if he wanted, but she hoped he'd slipped out when she ran to answer the door. The more distance between them, the better.

"Are you okay?" Jackson settled in beside her. "You're all jumpy."

His closeness in the semidarkness was disconcerting. Something in his manner was off, like he was trying too hard to comfort her, his movements and facial expressions a too-bright caricature of his usual self. "You try thinking you're being fire-bombed on your home turf." *And then come home to find a man you never wanted to see again hiding in your closet. That'll light up your nerve endings.* "What did you need my laptop for?"

"Mine's fried. I left it plugged in at the office, thinking I'd go back and finish some reports after dinner, but the storm had other plans. That was why I had to ditch on dinner. Lightning hit our building. Good thing all of the other computers were hooked to surge protectors. It looks like I'm the lucky one who got zapped."

"That's good." She went to work on the knot in her other boot, the pressure of the day deafening her so she heard only half of Jackson's story. Typically, his brotherly presence was comforting. Tonight, though, every word out of his mouth sliced cuts in her raw nerves.

"*That's good?* What is? That my computer got fried?" His voice wagged with amusement that didn't match the events of the day.

"No. That the others are okay." Cassidy jerked her shoelace. The knot grew tighter instead of working loose.

A soft scrape and a thud drifted in from the kitchen, and Jackson looked up, tensed as if to spring. "Did you hear that?"

"Hear what? It was nothing." Let it be the sound of Shane leaving her life forever. Nobody would hear her complain about that.

Jackson snatched the flashlight from the coffee table and stood. "Was the power off when you got home?"

"Yes, but—"

"And did you get a cat since I was last here?" He eased toward the door to the kitchen, voice lowered.

"No." Cassidy rocketed off of the couch. Jackson couldn't go in there and find Shane sneaking his way out the door. There was no telling what he'd think. "I'm sure it's—"

"Somebody's in your house," he whispered as he edged toward the kitchen.

"Jackson!" Her voice held all of the authority she normally reserved for wayward privates. "There is nobody in my house." Why was she protecting Shane? As soon as she figured out why he was camping out in her closet, she'd probably call the police just to prove her point. If she did that, though, it would bring the authorities—and her chain of command when they got wind of it—into her personal life. The sigh that escaped was a fitting punctuation mark at the end of this day. It wasn't worth the hassle.

Jackson hesitated, bobbing the beam of the flashlight in her direction, his expression dark in the reflected beam from the light. "Are you sure?"

"I came in that way. And nobody could get from anywhere else in the house to the kitchen without walking right past us." Cassidy perched on the edge of the couch and hoped her voice was convincing as she reached for her bootlace.

Annoyed indecision flickered on Jackson's face in the dim light. "What are you playing at, Matthews?"

Since when did he refer to her by her last name? "The only thing I'm 'playing at' is too much adrenaline and not enough food in my system, okay?"

With a last glance toward the kitchen, he walked over to the couch, settled the flashlight onto the table, and sat down next to her again. His eyes stayed on her, probing. "And you're one hundred percent sure you're okay?"

"I'm fine." She jerked the laces free and yanked her boot off her foot, fighting the sudden urge to throw it at her friend. This day—and the man in her kitchen—had gone to her head.

"Uh-huh. You act like everything's perfectly normal."

Well, let's see. A toasted Honda. Her ex hiding in her house. Everyone in her life going cuckoo at once. Yeah, normal was all over her house. "Too much went down in too many places today."

"Other than things going boom?"

"It's like my whole life went boom." Cassidy pressed her big toes together. It was too hard to breathe while split in two, her thoughts in one room and her body in another.

He eyed her like he had something to say, then pressed his lips together and stood. As he shouldered her bag, he said, "Thanks for digging this out of your car for me. I can bring it to you Monday morning." Jackson pulled the door open and paused with one foot inside and one on the concrete of the front porch. "You sure you don't want me to check out what went bump in your kitchen?"

"It was nothing. And I've been to war. Three times. I can take care of myself in my own house."

He flipped a mock salute as the streetlights flickered on behind him and her AC unit hummed to life.

"See? Nothing to worry about." Cassidy gripped the doorknob tightly and willed Jackson to leave before she told him about Shane or said anything else she'd regret in the morning.

He tossed a wave in her direction without looking back and wasn't halfway down the sidewalk before Cassidy shut the door and bolted for the kitchen. If Shane was still in that closet, he had a lot of explaining to do, then he'd have to get out of her life forever. The last thing she needed was his messing with her head. And he was definitely messing with her head.

Slipping in her socks on the tile, she gripped the door handle to steady herself, then yanked the closet open. Only her coats stared back at her. Shane was gone.

Shane ground his teeth together as he sat at the old wooden kitchen table while his roommate Derek Mann, a retired Special Forces buddy, practiced his rusty medic skills on the slash wound across his triceps.

"Logan, you're lucky Cassy didn't knife you herself. Unless she did, and you invented the whole story about somebody prowling around her house just so you could save some face." For a moment, silence held court in the small bachelor apartment. "You got bested by a girl, didn't you?"

Standing next to her today had definitely gotten the best of him in ways he'd thought he was long past. "Yeah," Shane exhaled in a rush. "You caught me." He winced as Derek applied alcohol to the injury and tried to focus on the flat-screen TV mounted on the wall. The late news flashed the photo of a Fort Bragg soldier killed in Afghanistan. Shane's gaze drifted to the brown leather couch instead. He'd seen enough death to last twenty lifetimes. "I think getting gashed was probably less painful than being bludgeoned by the Maglite she was swinging." He twisted his head around to check on Derek's progress. "She meant business."

Dark-skinned fingers forced his face to turn away, though Derek never shifted his attention from his work. "Dude, you know it hurts worse if you watch. Let me handle it. The stitching won't be as pretty as if you had a real doc take care of it, but it won't be infected and you won't have to answer any probing questions, all right? You're lucky the dude had bad coordination."

"'The dude had bad coordination?'" Shane smiled in spite of the pain. "Man, I have mad self-defense skills. I sent the ol' boy packing."

"So why did you end up hiding in a closet?"

"Cut a guy some slack, would you?" Shane flinched as the first poke of the needle pierced skin. He bit back a groan. "He bolted when she opened the garage door, and I had nowhere else to go."

"Why did you go to the house anyway? You know you convinced her a long time ago you're a bottom dweller."

"She was convinced because I was." Shane swallowed another dose of pain, although this one had nothing to do with his arm. "Back then." The silence stretched out, heavy and medicine-laden, as Shane thought about how he'd treated Cassy, how the arrogance rooted in his then-new assignment to Special Forces had changed him. The drinking. The late-nights hanging out with his buddies. The weekends he hadn't bothered to come home at all. He couldn't decide which burned more, the alcohol that seared his arm or the guilt that blazed in his gut. He glanced at Derek's work.

"If you're out to make her believe you're not the same guy anymore, then you've got your work cut out for you. I doubt she's gonna buy that Jesus made you different the very first time you tell her." Derek dug through the first aid kit until he found a roll of white gauze, which he ripped with his teeth. "But, dude, what in the world were you thinking? You don't woo a girl by breaking and entering."

"The last thing I want is to *woo* her." Even as he said it, he started to wonder if it still held true. Shane shook his head against the thought and against the sting in his arm. It had to be true. He couldn't tangle himself up with her again. It had hurt too badly to watch their years together implode the first time. "Maybe I was a jerk, but she didn't give me a chance to redeem myself. She just threw everything away without looking back. I don't need that kind of grief."

"True. So, tell me, if Cassy didn't cut you, who did?"

Shane tilted his chin and leveled his gaze on Derek's. "You're getting pushy in your old age."

"Just don't appreciate buddies taking hits when they aren't in a war zone." The matter-of-fact words didn't gibe with the concern in the dark eyes.

Shane shifted and ran his free hand through his hair. "I don't appreciate it either."

Derek taped the bandage into place and repacked his supplies. "Well, you can act the fool about this if you want. Your life."

"Yep. And I don't need you playing father figure, old man." Shane's voice strained as he pulled his arm in front of him to inspect his bandaged triceps. Now that it was sewn and wrapped, the throbbing didn't seem as insistent as it had earlier. A few ibuprofen ought to take the edge off, but pain was the least of his worries. Cassy and he were both in the crosshairs and there was no time to hide before the trigger was pulled.

* * *

After a hot shower and a change into sweats, Cassidy felt the day recede. Still, she found herself back in front of the closet. She opened the door again and stared into it. Lots of coats, but no Shane. She tapped her finger against her thigh and tried to decide if she should be worried or angry.

Definitely angry. Exactly what had he been thinking, hiding in her closet? Posttraumatic stress disorder must have kicked in for him. Maybe she should call a therapist. Then again, why should she even care? His problems weren't hers anymore. Let whatever girl he decided to flirt with this week deal with it. Forget it. She kicked her foot out, and the closet door slammed with a satisfying *bang*.

The paper bag that held the squashed remains of her hamburger rested in the corner, ketchup and chili oozing in grease slicks on the paper. Yeah, that would make a wonderful meal. She made a face and leaned down to scoop up the dinner that was now destined to feed the trash can. A ketchup smudge a few feet from the bag caught her eye, and she swiped it with her finger.

The spot smeared and Cassidy froze, her stomach twisting. Blood. Two droplets splotched the vinyl between the closet and the door to the garage. Narrowing her eyes, she backtracked, eyes scanning the linoleum as she went. There. Several long smears streaked the floor in the hallway between the kitchen and the dining room.

She gulped back nausea and leaped up to yank open the door to the garage, sudden panic fueling her desire to see with her own eyes Shane wasn't somewhere bleeding to death. "Shane!" Her shout fragmented against the garage door and shattered against her eardrums. Silence followed. Easing down the steps, she flipped on the light. Her numb fingers fumbled with the door that led to the backyard before she managed to unlock it and step out. Wet grass clung to her bare feet. The gate to the privacy fence hung open, but the yard was still. No shadows shifted. No leaves rustled in the stagnant air behind the earlier rainstorm.

Cassidy clicked the gate shut and wandered into the house, wondering where Shane had gone and just how badly he was injured. Securing the garage door behind her, she tried to shake off the image of him in this kitchen. It was clear he was gone again. She needed to forget him.

But some small corner of her soul still cared enough to worry. The image of his face, illuminated by her flashlight beam, froze on the movie screen in her mind.

Cassidy shook her head. No. He'd left. And she had no way to find him, no idea who to contact. She hadn't even realized he was stationed at Bragg. It would only make her look foolish if she called the police and said her bleeding ex-husband had vanished from her coat closet. Maybe she'd hallucinated the whole thing. Gripping her forehead between her thumb and index finger, she stared at the floor and tried to beat back the headache that pounded behind her left eyeball.

Food. She needed to eat something.

She glanced at the linoleum. No, first she needed to clean the tile. Then she could eat something. Why had she stored the floor cleaner under the bathroom sink? She fluttered on the edge of weariness before pivoting on one heel and heading for the stairs in the den. As her foot landed on the bottom step, she paused, head tilted to one side.

A shoe print tattooed the carpet pile of the third step.

Cassidy rested her left foot beside the imprint. Much too big to be hers.

Her hand felt for the gun holstered at her hip, and she bit back a groan. No weapon. She no longer lived in a war zone and no longer carried a pistol. Pressing her lips together, she tiptoed into the living room, snatched the flashlight from the coffee table and crept up the stairs, pseudoweapon raised. Life in Afghanistan sure hadn't been this complicated. At least there, she'd had a gun and she'd known who the bad guys were.

Cassidy paused outside the door of the guest room at the top of the stairs. Silence filtered into the hallway. The beam of the flashlight swung across the room. No footprints marred the vacuum tracks in the carpet of the rarely used room.

At the door to her office, she changed tactics. Inhaling deeply, she flipped on the overhead light and stood ready to attack or defend. Instead, she froze. The only thing in its rightful place was the computer. Everything else—files, letters, bills, photos—was thrown around the room like the aftermath of an Iraqi dust storm.

A slow burn smoldered through her body, and it pulsed with her rising heartbeat. Shane. Clearly, he'd been looking for something, and he sure wasn't hurt badly enough to let a little blood stop him.

All sympathy evaporated. Whatever Shane wanted, she hoped he'd found it, because it was certain he would never again set one foot in her life to look for it.

THREE

The lid to the trash can thumped into place, and Cassidy whacked it with the side of her fist for good measure. She'd spent the sleepless predawn hours sorting through papers and setting her office in order. While the cleaning bug gripped her, she boxed everything she could find to donate to charity and bagged what was left for a trip to the landfill.

She stared at the bags and shoved her bangs off her forehead. This purge should have happened years ago. Now the accumulated junk, coupled with angry energy that fueled a full summer cleaning spree, meant she'd need something bigger than her SUV to get all of the usable items to a donation site.

The low hum of an engine drew her attention to the road. As if her thoughts had solidified into physical reality, a gray late-model pickup stopped in front of the house. Adrenaline tingled her fingertips at the sight of the vehicle, but it surged on a bullet when Shane climbed out of the cab. The dark jeans and forest green T-shirt he sported today proved it wasn't just the uniform that made the man.

Cassidy swallowed twice before her voice agreed to cooperate. "You have trouble with the words *stay away?*"

Shane stopped halfway between the truck and the house. His stance spoke of uncertainty. They'd known each other since high school, were together from the first day they met in English class until the day he walked out of her life, and the only other time she'd seen his confidence crack was the day he'd asked her to marry him.

She bit her lip and glared at the sky, shoving the memory of a mountain breeze and a diamond ring into the deepest well of her soul.

"Cassy, we need to talk."

"No, we don't. I'm confident you've got nothing new to say." She yanked her hands from her hip pockets and brushed them together before planting them on her hips. "Know what? I'm too tired to talk. I spent the past few hours cleaning the mess you made upstairs." She tilted her head toward the line of garbage bags against the wall. "You'd better hope whatever it was you were looking for isn't in there because it's out the door this afternoon." Turning her back on him, she stomped into the garage. *Good riddance to bad rubbish.* The corner of Cassidy's mouth twitched. Her grandmother's favorite brush-off had never been so appropriate.

"You're still angry?"

Without asking for permission, her feet planted and refused to take another step. Her spine went rigid, and a flush washed across her face and down the back of her neck. His question forced her to replay her reasons, to drag out old memories, to poke at her emotions and gauge their response. The hurt didn't take her breath away like it had when she'd signed her name to papers that wiped away the promises of a lifetime, but it was still there, needling her heart. She swallowed hard. "What do you think?"

When Shane spoke again, his voice was closer. "What do you mean by the mess I made upstairs? I didn't make it past the kitchen last night."

The change of subject jerked her thoughts sideways as she whirled and met green eyes mere inches from her own. Her heart thudded to a stop, then pounded an extra beat. He used to be the safest place she'd ever known, the solid ground she set her feet on. The way he stood so close now made her long for that security again. Try as she might, she couldn't force the longing aside.

"Tell me what happened, Cassy." Shane's voice rumbled low and played a melody on her heartstrings. She wasn't sure if he was asking about what happened upstairs or about what happened between them. Whichever it was, this was a song she didn't want to hear.

With more effort than she'd ever had to exert in her life, Cassidy stepped back and put a good six feet between them. "You trashed my office. Why? After all this time, what could you possibly be looking for?"

Shane ran his hand along his jaw, and his eyes flashed. "It wasn't me."

"Sure it wasn't. Some mythical dragon stormed into my house, and you're my knight in shining armor."

He reached for her, but she backed another step away, her foot whacking the step that led to the kitchen door.

"I didn't go upstairs last night, okay?" He pressed his lips together and exhaled through his nose. "I came here to tell you something's going on in your unit and—"

"And you thought you'd dig through all of my stuff instead? Maybe take out some ten-year-old aggression on my file drawer?"

"No." The word was firm enough to silence her protests and strong enough to tell her he hadn't bothered to listen to a word she'd said. Some things never changed. "I came here to talk some sense into you and instead found the guy who torched that kid's car in your parking lot." When she opened her mouth to speak, he took a step closer and buried her planned protest under his words. "Short and sweet, he's the one who was upstairs going through your stuff."

"And I suppose you threw down a fight with him in the kitchen and that was his blood I had to scrub off my floor last night? Please." Cassidy held up her hand to stem the flow of lies. "Surely you don't expect me to believe that. To begin with, Anderson's car blew up because he knows nothing about mechanical modifications. Now tell me, which movie did you steal your story from?" She rubbed her temples with her fingertips, overwhelmed by his reappearance in her orderly life. He brought up too many emotions, too many memories she didn't need to relive. "Know what? I was thinking last night I let you off too easy. Hiding in closets, Shane? Normal people don't do that. That's what stalkers and murderers and guys who can't let go do. I figured you were none of those things, but now I'm not so sure." Well, she was sure he was neither a stalker nor a murderer, but she wasn't so certain anymore about his ability to let her go.

Shane's eyes stared at a spot above her head, and she knew from past experience he worked hard to keep his frustration in check. After a second, he eased the left sleeve of his T-shirt to his shoulder and tilted his upper arm toward her. A heavy white bandage peeked out at her. "It's covering a knife wound. I got it in your kitchen, fighting off the guy who torched the car in your parking lot."

Cassidy's breath froze in her lungs. The blood had been real. Shane had been attacked. In her house. He could have been killed… Her hand raised to touch the bandage, but she caught herself and pulled it back. As she did, realization crept in.

Heated fear pooled at the base of her spine and softened her joints. Someone had been in her house. Someone had rifled through her things. Someone had waited for her to come home.

"There was…" Her knees refused to hold her up any longer, and she sank to the step, mind whipping through what could have happened if Shane hadn't been there. "Somebody else was here."

Shane knelt in front of her but didn't try to touch her. He opened his mouth, closed it, then ran his hand through his hair. "That's not all."

Cassidy swallowed her fear and sat straighter. No matter what else was going on, she refused to give Shane an inroad with her emotions, refused to let him smell her fear, even if he had piqued her curiosity and possibly saved her life. "Talk."

Never, not since the day he'd first laid eyes on her, had Shane wanted so badly to pull Cassy into his arms and keep her safe. The force of the emotion rocked him back on his heels. All he could do was stare at her and try to regain his balance. The late-morning sun filtered through the trees and softened everything about her. He'd never seen her look as vulnerable, as in need of a protector, as she did right now.

But he knew if he tried to touch her—especially with all of the anger simmering beneath the surface between them—he'd never get her to open her ears and listen.

He rocked forward and looked to her left, avoiding the direct confrontation contact with her hazel eyes always brought. "On my last mission in Afghanistan, we detained a guy in opium country because we believed he had intel about a Taliban leader we were trailing. He didn't, but he kept talking about parachutes. Every one of us figured he was just babbling scared and, after we checked him out, we let him go. Sent the intel up the food chain, washed our hands of it and moved on. Honestly, I forgot all about it. We wrapped up the mission and it never crossed my mind again."

"Okay." Cassy slid back on the stairs as though she tried to put as much distance between them as possible.

Shane ignored the sting of her rebuff. "One of the interpreters caught up with me a couple of weeks ago, while we were gearing up to return to the States. Said he couldn't understand what the parachute thing was all about, so he started digging. He even managed to find the guy we'd detained and asked him a few more questions." Shane rested his elbows on his knees and clasped his fingers. "Long story short, rumor has it among the locals somebody's been buying all of the opium they could get their hands on and working to smuggle it out of the country. Somebody associated with our military." He waited to see if she'd make the connection. The truth would have more impact if she put it together for herself.

It took a second, but her eyes widened and her lips parted. "Parachutes and our military? So that's why you think…"

Shane stood and jerked his neck to the side, trying to pop out some of the tension that had built across his shoulders. "The only unit handling parachutes in that area of the country at the time we detained the guy was—"

"Attached to the Eighty-Second."

He nodded and stared at the hot water heater in the corner of the garage. If he looked at her, he might not be able to resist pulling her off the step and sheltering her the only way he knew how. Some habits never died. "I don't have a good read on how, but the best I can figure, they're managing to get them in with the parachutes that come back here. It all sounded pretty out there to my thinking, so I figured I'd swing by the rigger shed, get the lay of the land and try to see if I could figure out who to trust before any more shipping containers came back."

"There are some coming in late next week. They should have come in yesterday, but they were delayed between here and Pennsylvania. One of the

GPS trackers isn't sending a signal, and the container is missing."

Shane's gut twisted. Everything was falling into place when he wanted it all to fall to pieces. "I was really hoping when I said that to you yesterday that you'd tell me it wasn't yours. They're coming from the depot in New Cumberland?"

She nodded.

If one of those containers truly had been tampered with, everything he suspected might be true. And that meant bigger trouble than he could even imagine.

Cassidy stood and brushed past him, walking toward the front of the garage. "You're hinting that some of my soldiers are running drugs. Under my nose." Suspicion laced her voice and stiffened her posture. "Too many people have their fingers in the pie when we ship gear to the States. And think about it. What soldier in their right mind would do such a thing? You buy drugs from those guys, you're funneling money straight to—"

"The very same guys who are shooting at you. I know." Shane swallowed hard, his pulse rate climbing as he studied the rough, unfinished wood of the step where she'd sat. If he couldn't get through to her, he had no ally. "Believe me, I know. You're giving them money for weapons and supplies and…" He balled his fists and fought the image of bloodied death as it tried to paint itself on his mind. It bled through his nightmares enough. He didn't need day terrors to go with it. His fists shook against his thighs. "That's the worst part. But you know guys out there have smuggled stuff back before. It makes me want to find the punk behind this and take care of it myself. Our money funding their bullets to shoot at my…at our soldiers…"

"If somebody's really doing what you say." Cassidy's low voice barely registered.

Shane dragged his focus to the immediate problem of keeping Cassy out of danger. "I don't know what else to tell you. The interpreter said they never referred to the guy by name. None of the people my man talked to had ever even seen him. And it gets worse." Shane looked over his shoulder, then pivoted to stare at her back. "This informant? He mentioned you. Well, the Division Parachute Officer. I'm not sure what they think it'll buy them, but…" He rolled his eyes to the ceiling and prayed in a way he couldn't quite put into words. He'd never wanted to be wrong so much in his entire life. "They're planning to smoke the Division Parachute Officer if things get crazy."

Cassy's breath caught. He could see it in the way she froze, her spine rigid.

"It is you, isn't it? You're the new DPO. That's why they hit your house."

She didn't move.

He'd hoped it wasn't her, that yesterday had been

a crazy, twisted coincidence. "Something must have happened. Something to force their hand. And I believe it's that shipping container disappearing. It's probably loaded." Shane took a deep breath. "I know this sounds like some made-up story. And if I were in your shoes, I wouldn't believe me either. But I've never lied to you, Cassy. I might have treated you horribly and left you on your own, but I never lied to you."

She stood with her back to him, staring at the street.

A group of kids raced by on bicycles. Their laughing shouts floated up the driveway and into the garage. Outside the door, life went on as normal. Inside, where he waited, everything twisted and jumbled like malfunctioning parachute lines. And there stood Cassy, her feet half in the normal world outside and half in the dysfunction in the garage.

"If this is true, why didn't you just call in the Criminal Investigation Division? Or call the police yesterday? Why break into my house?" She didn't look at him, but her back was as unbending as a rifle barrel.

"See it from my point of view. You think CID is going to drop everything because some scared informant coincidentally mentioned my ex-wife's job? They'd call me crazy and show me the door. Either that or they'd lock me up and label me a stalker. Like I said, we sent the initial information up the chain of command, but nothing ever happened. They didn't buy it then, why would they buy it now? That's why I had to check it out for myself. I need more."

A warm breeze whispered through the tops of the pine trees, but the garage remained silent as Cassy continued to stare straight ahead. She drew in a deep breath. "I don't know. This is all too incredible. It can't be real."

The words slammed into Shane's chest, and he dropped his arms to his sides. "What?"

Cassy didn't look at him. "How do I know this isn't some crazy, PTSD-induced fantasy you've cooked up? It sounds like something you might have seen in some action movie or read in one of those thrillers you were always so interested in. So…I don't know."

"Cassy." He took a step toward her, more desperate than he'd ever felt in his life. He wasn't asking her to take him back—would never ask her to take him back—but he needed her to trust him and let him help her get to the bottom of this business before she got hurt. He reached for her. "Let me help you."

She whirled on him, fury blazing from her eyes with such heat that it forced him to take a step back. "Who says I need help? You didn't want to help me before. Why on earth would you think I'd turn to you now? The only reason I didn't call the cops last night is because I know it would cost you your security clearance if you got arrested."

And the psych eval they'd put him through probably wouldn't help matters. "I appreciate the thought." It came out laced with more sarcasm than he'd intended, so he pushed forward before she could erupt. "The car. Come on, you can't tell me—"

She shoved her palm a bare inch from his face. "Stop. I told you. Anderson's car went sky high because he knows nothing about where to install a nitrous bottle."

"And I'm telling you I saw somebody light it."

"You blow any sort of credibility you have every time you say stuff like that."

"Stop it, Cassy." Shane looped his thumb and index finger around her wrist and pulled her hand away from his face. "You can play the denial game all you want, and we can rehash it until World War III breaks out, but it's never going to change the facts."

She jerked her arm from his light grasp. "Please just stop with the—" Her voice raised, then plummeted to a whisper, her gaze dropping to his hand, still extended toward her. "You're right. I just... wanted it to be simple."

"Can't fault you for that."

With a short shake of her head, she sank against the front of her Trailblazer and stared up at his face, her gaze digging into his. "You're telling the truth?" Her voice betrayed her. She was giving in.

Shane swallowed hard, his gut telling him he was

looking at his last shot to convince her she needed his help. "A hundred percent."

Cassy drew the corner of her lip into her mouth. It felt like the whole earth stilled when she exhaled. "Okay. What do we do now?"

FOUR

Cassidy fumbled the key to the outer office, studied it to make certain she had the right one and tried again. She couldn't get it to turn in the lock.

After a weekend of too much time with Shane, sorting through the mess in her office and nightmares peopled by shadowy assailants, Monday morning felt like a slog through hip-deep mud. She'd be lucky if she made it through her 0900 meeting without snoring. Leave it to Shane to show up unannounced and tilt her world after over a decade's absence just as things literally exploded around her. *Could use a little help here, God.* As if God were going to answer her. He was busy with His own agenda. If He was into answering prayers, her father would still be alive, and her life would look a whole lot different.

The keys slipped from her fingers and clattered to the floor. "Really?" She closed her eyes and leaned her forehead against the door. It was 0445, too early for anyone else to be in. Surely no one would know if she took a nap right here in the stairwell with her cheek smashed against the door frame.

Hands clamped onto her shoulders.

Cassidy's breath caught mid-inhale, and she choked on the air trapped in her throat. Her muscles tightened, paralyzing her. Why hadn't she let Shane come with her instead of telling him to show up later?

"Cass, calm down."

Jackson's voice cut through her panic, loosened the blockage in her throat, and allowed the air to leak out. Her muscles relaxed as she gulped a breath. "What is with the entire world sneaking up on me lately?" And when had her guard dropped so much that she let them?

Confusion flashed across Jackson's features as he shook his head. "Who else is sneaking up on you?"

"Don't worry about it. Sorry." Cassidy bent and retrieved her key ring from the floor. "I'm running on no sleep. Again. It's becoming a bad habit."

Jackson took the keys from her hand and dealt with the lock, then followed her across the outer office to open her door. "So I see. Lucky for you, I come bearing gifts." He held out a grape soda and tilted the bottle lazily back and forth, a slight smile tipping the corners of his mouth. "C'mon. You know you want to say yes."

She snatched the soda from his hand and cracked

it open, tension easing as purple carbonation hit the back of her throat.

"There's another bad habit you need to break," Jackson said. "You enjoyed that first sip a little too much."

"So says my supplier." Cassidy frowned at the reference. Suppliers. Smugglers. Drugs. The weekend's stress rushed back into her body and put down stakes in her temples, intent on camping out for a while. "Thanks, but you can't stay," she said. "The last thing I need is for Colonel Fryar to step in here and think I'm fraternizing with…you." She grinned to soften the words and to hide her fears. "Thanks for the sugar rush, though."

"Is there such a thing as contractor fraternization?" Jackson unlocked the second door, followed her into her office and leaned one elbow on the gray metal filing cabinet next to the door. "Fine. I know when I'm not wanted. Glad you appreciate fine beverages, but that's not why I'm here." He slipped her laptop case off of his shoulder. "I told you I'd get this back to you today."

"Thanks, but you could have waited. That's my personal one, not my army-issued one. If this tells you anything about how my weekend went, though, I totally forgot you had it." Guilt kept her from looking him in the eye. It shouldn't bother her she wasn't telling Jackson the whole story—and really, why wasn't she?—but the gnawing on her conscience didn't ease. Cassidy rounded her desk and busied herself sorting the files in her in-box. Shane had gotten into her head. Jackson was a friend. There was no reason to treat him like a buzzing gnat, especially when the sight of him lent an uneasy sense of safety to her jagged nerves.

Jackson crossed his arms over his chest. "I'll keep your little insomnia-induced amnesia a secret if you'll let me make good on dinner tonight because I ditched you Friday. Unless you're still too tired to carry on a conversation. Come on, Cass. Throw me a line."

"Hmm." Cassidy drew circles on the keyboard of her desktop computer, her finger orbiting the E key, which was almost entirely rubbed off from use. Every phrase that zipped through her mind sounded cliché or hurtful. Of course, she could always go for the totally original, *Well, my ex burned me so bad that I've never recovered and, by the way, he was hiding in my closet the other night when we were talking. With a stab wound. And the conviction that my life's in danger. Oh, and when he looked me in the eye, there's the slightest possibility my heart rate marched double-time.* Her cheeks warmed. Uh, no, it did not. It certainly did not.

She clicked the space bar twice. "Somebody broke into my house Friday night." It wasn't what she'd planned to say, but it sure might work as a conversation changer.

An unreadable look darkened Jackson's features, then he stepped toward her. "What? When?" He rounded the desk and gripped her upper arms, forcing her to look at him. "Did you see anything? Are you okay?"

Something about the way his fingers dug into her arms felt too possessive, too…demanding. This was not the way she wanted to be touched. She'd have preferred it if he'd pulled her into a comforting hug first and pressed for answers second, not the other way around.

"I'm fine." Cassidy pulled free from his grasp and resisted the strong urge to straighten her gray army T-shirt. "As far as I can tell, they only hit the upstairs and didn't take anything. Sha— I must have scared them off when I came home. And I don't have the first clue who it was." That was half true. She wasn't sure who'd torn through the upstairs, even though she knew who'd brought chaos into her life by showing his face downstairs.

Jackson stared at her for a long time. The look in his eye almost seemed like he was gauging her tone of voice, searching for something he couldn't quite put his finger on.

When Shane told her he wasn't responsible for the damage in her office, the first thing he'd wanted to do was hold her. No, he hadn't moved, but the desire had telegraphed straight from his eyes to her heart.

He had a protective instinct that still lingered. Time would tell if that was a good thing or a bad thing.

Jackson drew in a deep breath and flicked his eyes from her feet to her face as if to reassure himself she was fine. "You're really okay?"

"Other than I got no sleep this weekend, I'm fine."

"What did the police say?"

"Actually," Cassidy dropped her gaze to a memo on her desk. "I didn't call them." She braced herself for the lecture.

"You don't think it was your ex, do you?" Jackson leaned his hip against her desk and picked up a commander's challenge coin the colonel had given her as a thank-you after her last deployment. He studied the twin A's of the Eighty-Second Airborne All-American design on the front. "You heard from him lately?"

Cassidy focused on the coin in his hand. No questions about the police? And it was odd he'd brought up Shane because she'd mentioned him to Jackson only a handful of times over the past year. "Shane and I went our separate ways years ago. I'm reasonably certain he wasn't involved in ransacking my office." *Now don't ask me again if I've heard from him. Don't make me lie to you.*

Seeming satisfied, Jackson clattered the coin to the desk and stood. "I should go. I have to run diagnostics today and make sure the power surge we took really didn't do any damage. Maybe I'll try to talk someone higher up the ladder into buying us a few new computers."

A small part of her relaxed at his retreat. She couldn't take any more relationship questions, especially not today. One look at Shane had served as a stiff reminder of why she would never let herself endure love again. "Good luck with that. I'm pretty sure nobody's bought new computers in your building since 1986."

"That's because nobody else had my persuasive charm. I'm a convincing guy." Jackson stopped in the doorway and winked. "So…dinner?" The laid-back Jackson returned in full force.

Cassidy gave in. It was easier than coming up with yet another excuse, and she needed him out of here before Shane showed up. That confrontation involved more than she felt like explaining to either of them. "Sure."

"See you around 6:30?"

She nodded and watched him walk away before turning her attention to her computer. Forget Shane. Forget Jackson. Forget outrageous stories. Focus on the job at hand. She had just enough time to clear her email in-box before Shane showed up to see if he could spot something in her soldiers that familiarity wouldn't let her perceive. "Hey."

Cassidy jerked her head up to find Jackson in the doorway, dangling her keys from his fingers. "Can't get home to get ready for dinner without these."

"Thanks." She held up her hand, and he tossed the keys to her, then disappeared. "There is no way this can get any more complicated," she muttered, sliding her ID card into the common access card reader on the computer. She punched the power button and sat back, sipping grape soda and fixing a blank stare on the screen.

Forgetting was impossible. Shane had reappeared, sounding like he had a case of the crazies. Jackson abruptly wanted more. What was going on with the men in her life? Any second now, her stepfather would call and tell her he'd decided to become a Russian cosmonaut. That was just about the only way her life could get any weirder.

She clicked *Okay* on the "For Government Use Only" warning box, then rotated the soda bottle between her palms, eyes narrowed. Maybe she was the one on the crazy train. That would have to be it if she thought for an instant her heart had picked up speed over Shane Logan of all people.

A window she'd never seen before popped onto the screen. Setting her soda aside, Cassidy leaned forward and read aloud. "Error *123, could not read supplied card." Her voice drawled into what sounded awfully close to a whine that grated on her own nerves. "Come on." She closed the window, reached across her desk and wiggled her ID card in the reader, then tried again, eyes scanning the screen. "Yes, you can read the 'supplied card.' You just read it on Friday, stupid machine."

With a sigh so harsh it rippled the papers on her desk, she yanked her card out of the reader and rubbed the chip against the leg of her physical training shorts, then shoved it back into place and waited. *Three invalid log in attempts.* Three? No. One. The one just now. Cassidy rapped the mouse against the desk. "Seriously? You're a male now, too? You've lost your mind on me like the rest of them?"

Nope. She was the one who looked as though her mind had taken flight, talking out loud to this poor excuse for a paperweight.

She dropped her forehead against her palm and swallowed her irritation. It was going to take more than a twenty-ounce bottle of sugar water to get her through this day without a major blowup. Insomnia and Shane-fueled agitation swirled just under the surface. Cassidy fiercely hoped no unsuspecting soldier tripped up in front of her today. The full force of her frustration would probably send them to their branch officer to beg for a trip to Afghanistan.

She was practicing her own version of deep-breathing exercises when Shane's voice washed over her. "I see you still talk to yourself."

The heat of intimate familiarity pricked the back of her neck and melted her hands to the keyboard. Cassidy straightened and waved him in. "I...didn't hear you come in."

"Probably because you were busy talking to your computer friend there." He sank into the chair across from her. "Something wrong?"

She swatted the CAC reader with the back of her hand and ignored the way her breath stuck in her chest. "Stupid piece of junk claims my ID card's invalid. After this weekend, I'm starting to think I have sojourned into the land of confusion."

"Welcome to the army."

Rolling her eyes, Cassidy sat back in her chair. "You're early. I thought we said nine."

Shane shrugged and toyed with the Velcro on his leg pocket. "Knew you'd be here alone and didn't like the idea, especially not right now."

The meaning behind the words rolled from Cassidy's ears to the center and marched double-time against her chest. Before her own words could form, movement at the door drew Cassidy's eye. Master Sergeant McIntyre filled the doorway, his eyebrow arched in question. "Mac." Cassidy stood as Shane glanced over his shoulder to follow her gaze, then rose to his feet. "Mac, this is Major Shane Logan. Major Logan, this is Master Sergeant McIntyre. The major's here to…" She stuttered to a halt. Why exactly was Shane here? To interrogate her soldiers? To snoop around the rigger shed? There was no really good way to explain his presence.

"I'm here to visit." Shane extended his hand and clasped Mac's, then gestured to the chair beside his and dropped back into his seat. "If you need the chief, you're not interrupting anything."

Cassidy fought to keep her eyes from narrowing as she caught a hint of what Shane was up to. The whole routine of inviting Mac in reeked of checking the older man out, feeling to see if he was involved in the trouble. Overwhelmed by a fierce desire to defend the one coworker she trusted implicitly, she bit her tongue, then reconsidered. She was too close to the situation. The reason Shane was here was to be an objective observer, something she'd just proven to herself she could never be. She sighed and gave a slight nod, letting Mac know it was okay to speak freely in front of Shane.

The master sergeant stepped into the room and stood behind the empty chair. "I was just going to tell you I got an email over the weekend. Shipping containers will be here Thursday. I wanted to take a look at next week's training schedule and see if we need to juggle anything. You have one handy? I thought mine was on my desk, but somebody must have snagged it."

Cassidy wrinkled her forehead. "Why would somebody do something so pointless as to take that? It's posted on the board for the world to see."

"Beats me, but…"

The gravity of the older man's voice brought a halt to Cassidy's questions. Something bigger than a training schedule took up space in his words. She

Freefall

dropped her hands palms-down onto the desk and tried to force down rising dread. "There's more?"

At her question, Shane straightened in his seat, his features hardening. He'd heard it, too, that timbre that said something wasn't quite right.

"Maybe, maybe not." McIntyre settled onto the edge of the standard-issue gray army chair and rested his elbows on his knees, his maroon beret dangling from his fingers. "The thing is, I know the training schedule was on my desk. I had it out Friday afternoon to give it a last look before I took off for home. And things were out of place in the office when I got in today."

Fear and suspicion mingled and pricked the back of Cassidy's neck. She swallowed nausea and the bubble of fear that whispered Shane's words from over the weekend. She flicked a glance in his direction, then looked back to Mac. "Like?"

"Probably nothing. A couple of my files were moved. And you can tell from the line of dust on my desk that my in-box isn't sitting where it used to be."

Cassidy smiled in spite of herself. "Need me to find a drill sergeant to come in here and give you a basic refresher on cleaning techniques?"

"You need me to get a white glove and run it across the top of *your* desk?"

A grin flashed onto Cassidy's face, then faded. "I can make it even more interesting." She rested a hand on her computer's monitor. "My machine's telling me I've had too many invalid log in attempts."

"Could be unrelated." Mac shook his head even as the words left his mouth. "But my gut tells me there's something not kosher about all of this."

And her gut fought the idea with every combative technique she knew.

Shane sat forward in his chair to meet Mac's eye. "You're sure it's not just about somebody needing a training schedule?"

"Well," Mac hesitated, clearly unsure if it was okay to air his thoughts to this stranger. "Like the chief said, there's one posted for the world to see. And I can't count how many copies of it are floating around the shed at any given time." He turned his attention to Cassidy. "And even if somebody wanted mine specifically for some reason, it was top center on my desk. No need to go digging."

Cassidy wriggled uncomfortably in her chair, converging theories circling in her head. She didn't like to think this had anything to do with what Shane suspected. What he was talking about was more than simple smuggling. Buying drugs from Afghan nationals was as good as funneling money straight to the Taliban, and aid to the enemy in any form equaled treason.

Forget treason. As far as she was concerned, it equaled murder. "It could have been somebody looking for quick cash." Even a thief in their ranks was preferable to one of her soldiers doing business with the enemy.

"Nope. That's what I thought at first, and that's what's weird about it. I keep a little money in my top desk drawer for vending machines. It's still there."

On a hunch, Cassidy reached down and pulled open her center desk drawer. Her loose change rested where it always sat. "Same here. Looks like it's all there, too."

"So nothing's missing off your desk?" Shane stood and paced to the office door, staring out as he waited for her answer.

"Not that I've noticed. Then again, my office is locked separately. It would be harder to access." She flipped through papers and folders, then yanked one free and held it out to Mac. "Here's my copy of the training schedule." She narrowed her eyes as he took the paper, then shuffled a few more folders, her nerve endings growing colder by the second. *No. Let anything be missing but...* "Oh, no." Her hands dropped to her sides, cold and numb.

Shane was in front of her desk faster than she could blink. "What?"

"Friday morning, right before all of the excitement, I got an email from the Unit Movement Officer in charge of packing the missing container. He wanted me to take a look at the weights on our pallets. Said they were different on the return trip than some of the others." The soda she'd swigged earlier threatened to make a reappearance as dots connected to form a menacing image. "I printed it out and left it on my desk. When everything went crazy, I forgot all about it. It's gone."

McIntyre drew his eyebrows together. "An inventory and a training schedule? Makes no sense."

"Makes perfect sense to me," Shane muttered, shoving his hands into his pockets.

"I'm sorry." Mac stood and squared off with Shane. "Would one of you explain what's going on here?"

Cassidy scrambled. Even though she trusted Mac, right now was not the time to let trust rule the day. She needed to default to part of the truth, and fast. "It's not just your desk, Mac. Somebody broke into my house looking for something. Shane is…an old friend. It's possible there's a tie between what's happening here and at my house, and he's helping me look into it."

"Somebody broke into your house?" Mac's shoulders relaxed as he turned to Cassidy. "You okay?"

She nodded. Her *coworker* asked if she was okay. So where was Jackson's head?

"They take anything?"

"Not as far as I could tell. It would have been easy to take the computer or loose cash, but they didn't." She flicked a finger at the pens in a cup on her desk. "I went through everything, and I can't tell anything's missing."

"You call the police?"

"No." Cassidy hesitated. She didn't really want to share all of Shane's suspicions. "And it doesn't matter. I can't call them now because I already cleaned the room. There's nothing to see."

"You know I want to lecture you about the whole police thing, right?" Mac turned back to Shane. "Talk some sense into her?"

Shane bit back a smile as he nodded.

Cassidy flared her nostrils. She could take care of herself. And she was in the room. What was it about men that made them default to treating women like they were helpless or even invisible?

With a quick glance at his watch, Mac said, "It's about time for PT formation. Want to continue this later?"

"If we have to. But we can skip the lecture, if that's okay with you. Go on downstairs. I'll be there in a few."

Shane waited for Mac to disappear before he spoke. "Now what? You can't deny something's up."

"I'm not denying it. I just want you to be wrong."

"I'm not."

"I know."

"Look." Shane tapped his index finger on the edge of her desk. "Do you mind if I take a look at your training schedule? Maybe something's there that shouldn't be."

"Don't know what it could be. It's a glorified calendar. There can't be anything earth-shattering on it." She stretched a hand out to pick up the paper, then stopped. "I gave mine to Mac. There's always a copy posted on the board downstairs. You can run down and see if it's still there. If I'm not here when you get back, I'll be at S-6 trying to get help for my computer."

Shane nodded and straightened, slapping his beret against his thigh. "We'll figure this out. You know that, right?"

Cassidy shrugged and waited for him to leave, then slumped in her seat. When did she take the leap down the rabbit hole? First Anderson's car made like fireworks, then Shane jumped out of her coat closet and everything got weirder from there. Nothing made sense, and the very idea someone would risk trouble just to steal a training schedule had to be the most ludicrous thing yet. It was like staring at a jigsaw puzzle with all of the pieces sanded down. Nothing fit together.

FIVE

Cassidy leaned against the wall and looked at her watch, then back at the door. If Shane wanted any part of this, he'd better hurry. He'd vanished after their short talk in her office, probably going to watch all of her soldiers come in for physical training.

The S-6—in charge of all things technical around the battalion—was Captain Foster. But one of the guys in the shop just so happened to be Private Anderson, owner of the crisped Honda. Sheer coincidence, she was sure.

Anderson had exactly seven minutes before 0630 physical training formation, but he was well-known for squeaking in at the buzzer, usually bleary-eyed from an all-night gaming session and amped on whatever energy drink was handy at the moment. Maybe all that screen time made him better at the tech stuff he dealt with. It might do the kid good to see if all of his video games could constitute a tax write-off.

She peeked at her watch again. Six more minutes.

Yeah, it was going to take lots of caffeine to get her through this day.

She hadn't shared Shane's story or her growing suspicions with McIntyre, but she'd have to soon. He was already starting to ask questions. The issue was a growing paranoia that left her wondering who she could trust. If one of her soldiers was up to something worse than she could have ever conjured, there was no way to tell who the culprit was, what they were after or even who she could trust. It was easier to believe her ex-husband had jumped off the insanity cliff than it was to think her soldiers were cutting drug deals with Afghan warlords. Problem was, all of the evidence stacked in Shane's favor, and as far-fetched as it all was, she had to believe him.

And now she began to wonder if the break-in at her house had more to do with her computer than a destructive search.

She straightened, and her booted foot thudded to the floor, whacking a tremor through her knee. If her timing wasn't off, then the power had gone out while the intruder was in her office. What if the target really was her computer and everything went dark before whoever it was had a chance to manipulate any files?

"What are you doing?"

The unexpected words jolted Cassidy out of her reverie and yanked words from her throat. "Shane?"

Her nostrils flared. "Would you please stop sneaking up on me?"

"Well, stop confronting people without backup. That's what you were about to do, right?"

Cassidy didn't want to notice the way his uniform made his eyes seem greener. Spacing her heels at shoulder-width, she straightened and attempted to stare Shane down, even though she had to look up to do so. "I told you I was coming down here. And I'm not 'confronting' anybody. I'm asking a private in my S-6 shop to take a look at my computer."

Before he could answer, Private Anderson appeared. His step stuttered when he spotted Cassidy and Shane. There was a brief hesitation, then he squared his shoulders and stepped between them to the door.

Shane eyed her over Anderson's shoulder and dipped his head toward the younger man, skepticism staining his face. "The kid whose car blew up," he mouthed.

Cassidy nodded. So she'd left that bit of information out.

"That's no coincidence," he muttered. With a casual air that had to be an act, he leaned one shoulder against the wall and settled in to watch her interaction with the younger soldier.

Private Anderson focused on opening the door, the heavy scent of laundry soap from freshly washed PT clothes wafting in a cloud around him. Somebody needed to take the kid in hand and teach him how much detergent was too much. "Did you need something, Chief?" he asked, hefting his bag and shoving the door open.

"Sure do, Anderson." She followed him into the office and watched him drop his duffel bag while he tried to balance his uniform under one arm. She could feel the heat of Shane behind her, even though he had stopped just inside the doorway. "Find out anything about your car this weekend?"

"Yeah. Um, I mean, yes, ma'am." Anderson dropped a combat boot beneath his desk and knelt to pick it up, then shoved both boots into the duffel bag. "They... They want me to fax them the official report."

My word, the kid was antsy this morning. It wasn't something she could fault him for. Shane's presence had her composure twanging like banjo strings. "Something wrong, Private?"

"Oh. No, ma'am. Just not expecting you to be waiting for me. Can I help you with something, Chief?" Anderson pulled at the neck of his gray T-shirt and tugged at the hem of his black shorts. He finally seemed to notice Shane, glancing quickly at the rank on his chest. "Or you, sir?"

Cassidy allowed her suspicions to evaporate and tried not to smile. Anderson was fairly new to the unit, and sometimes younger soldiers weren't certain how to act around their superiors. Salute? Stand at attention? Follow every other sentence with ma'am or chief? Her nurturing female instinct urged her to back off a little, but the leader in her knew she shouldn't. "As a matter of fact, you can help me with a computer issue."

Behind her, Shane shifted. She could hear the scrub of his ACU material. He stepped closer, his presence squeezing the air from her lungs. Couldn't he just stay in his own personal space?

"A—a computer issue?" Anderson's voice pitched an octave higher, then his face burned red. "I mean, sure I can. Yes, ma'am. What's the problem?"

Cassidy willed her thoughts away from Shane. For a few breaths, she studied Anderson. Question after question tangled in her head, but caution stopped her. "Well, if I knew—"

"You wouldn't need me?" His posture relaxed. "Sure. How soon do you need it? I've got some other upgrades to finish, but if you're in a hurry I can get to it after PT."

Ah, so that was the problem. He knew he was late. Cassidy supposed she'd be a little antsy, too. Late for formation was punishable, and Anderson had skated that line one too many times. "Don't worry about formation. I'll talk to your section leader about why you're late."

"Formation? Oh. Yeah." Anderson fixed his attention on the floor at her feet. "So, when did you want me to get to your computer?"

"Whenever you get a chance is fine. I've got my army-issued laptop with me if I need to type something in a…" Her laptops. She hadn't even considered her laptops could be vulnerable.

A groan tried to work its way into open air. Before she realized she was doing it, she glanced over her shoulder at Shane.

The set of his jaw said his thoughts raked through the possibilities of everything she'd just said. Shane had a tactical mind, good at connecting the dots. Her conversation with Anderson would be more than enough to tip him off to her newly formed suspicions.

Cassidy turned away and focused on the kid in front of her. One thing at a time. "Know what? Whenever you get to it is fine, as long as it stays in my office. I don't want it walking off anywhere. And I want to be there when you come in."

"Yes, ma'am." Anderson looked like he was ready to snap a salute. "Anything else?"

"That'll do it." Cassidy turned and brushed past Shane, intent on the door. Her shoulder brushed his biceps, and the contact tingled at the base of her spine. This was the last thing she—

"Chief?" Anderson's voice sliced her thoughts.

She stopped but didn't look back. "Yes?"

"Any word on when that set of shipping containers is coming in?"

Cassidy's stomach dropped to the steel toes of her boots. Dates like that were none of his concern.

Before she could ask, Shane stepped in. "You have a need to know, Private?"

The dam holding back Cassidy's emotions splintered, and the most prevalent one was anger. Her building. Her soldier. He had no right to overstep her. None.

She opened her mouth to let loose a flood of admonition, but Shane held up his index finger behind his back. Cassidy ground her back teeth together. His knowing she was about to speak rankled her nearly as much as his reminder she didn't need to air personal thoughts in front of the younger soldier.

The private cleared his throat. "I have a new girlfriend, sir. I didn't know if they came in late if we'd have to stay after close of business to unload."

The air trapped in Cassidy's chest left her body in a rush. "They'll be here this week. Thursday, most likely."

"Will we be unloading them the day they come in?"

"If they get in early enough." She pivoted on one heel and pinned her gaze on Shane, ignoring the flurry of unease in her subconscious. "I think that's all I need. Major, if you'd like, we can finish our conversation outside."

Shane followed Cassy as she blasted down the hallway, her boots a staccato drumroll on the tile floor. She burst through the outside door with a crash and whirled on him after a quick survey of the parking lot revealed they were alone. Her hands shook, and he knew it took all of her discipline not to shove her finger in his face. "I would never dream of questioning one of your soldiers, no matter what the circumstances. If you're going to come around here and 'investigate' my people, we're going to lay some ground rules right now."

Some of the spark left Shane, and he winced. He'd disrespected her with that small step on her authority. Worse, he'd done it in front of one of her soldiers. "You're right. That was out of line."

His acquiescence seemed to steal the oxygen from her fury's fire. She froze as though her emotions had to switch gears, then relaxed and leaned back against the wall to stare across the parking lot. "Now what?"

Shane leaned a shoulder against the wall, careful to keep a safe distance. It seemed like he was the match to her fuse, and the more space between them the better. Never mind the fact that every time he got close, he only felt the need to get closer. "You think more than your work computer is involved."

She nodded. "I have four computers. The one at home, the one on the desk upstairs, my personal laptop and my government laptop. Somebody's for sure tampered with the one here, and I find it odd that everything in my home office was trashed except…"

Understanding shone light onto Shane's suspicions. "Except your computer. You said it was the only thing that wasn't touched. You think that was a blind. They messed with everything else to throw you off track."

"Bingo. So what could I have that somebody would want? The rigger shed isn't exactly a hotbed of classified activity. We inspect chutes and pack chutes and move them out. Busting into my computers couldn't possibly produce anything that would help somebody do something as physical as hiding drugs."

"Want me to come over after you get off work and take a look at the computer with you? Maybe there's something there you don't see." It was a risky question, but it would let him gauge whether she was truly ready to accept his help.

Cassy's face hardened for a moment, then softened into what looked like deliberate nonchalance. "I guess. Whatever. There's nothing there that I'd care if you—" She clenched her teeth and sucked in a quick breath. "Wait. I can't. I mean, later I can, like around nine or ten, but…I have plans."

Plans. Forget three guesses. He needed only one to figure out who lay at the center of those plans. His vision turned a murky green that he forced himself to blink away.

Before he could say a word, she dug into her

pocket and pulled out a key ring, which jingled as she twisted her house key free. "Here. I've got nothing to hide. You can see if there's anything there that rings any alarms to you. And it probably wouldn't hurt to have someone at the house because random people seem to like exploring when I'm not around."

Shane took the key, careful not to let his fingers brush hers. He didn't know what he thought would happen if they touched, but he just knew it would be combustible, one way or the other. He pocketed the key, then pivoted so that his back rested against the building, mimicking Cassy's posture. "Makes you wonder... Somebody breaks into your house and gets into a fight with me...a fight serious enough to involve a knife. I've got an interpreter who tells me soldiers are running drugs. You've got a car on fire in your parking lot, and now somebody's messing with your computers. It all seems really random."

"Too random."

"Yeah. With that much of a disconnect, you almost have to think it's deliberate, if that makes any sense. I mean, your only link is that the kid whose car blew up is also one of the guys who works on your computers, and that doesn't touch the interpreter's story." He frowned, remembering again how he'd stepped in front of her to question Private Anderson. Shane took a deep breath and shoved his hands into his pockets. "Look, I know it might be hard for you to understand why I went overboard. It's just… Nobody broke into my house and threatened my life. I want to know you're safe."

Cassidy's eyes met his and trapped him. The flicker he saw there reached inside him and drew up long-dormant emotions. They were emotions he'd never thought he'd have a need for again.

As quickly as the spark flared it died, and she shook her head. "No. You can poke around here and try to find out all you want about what this interpreter of yours told you, but I draw the line at letting you back into my personal life. I'll let you help on this, but it can't go beyond that. Once you've got enough evidence to go to the authorities, we're done." Pivoting on one heel, she yanked the door open and left him to watch her walk away, just as she had so many years ago.

All of his strength flowed into the pavement beneath his feet. Her refusal to trust him cut, especially because he knew he'd never done anything to destroy her faith.

Guilt lit a flame in the back of his neck. Once. Once he'd almost gone too far. On leave in a hometown bar, he'd disconnected a call to Cassy, frustrated by the walls between them, the time apart, the fact that marriage didn't seem to be the way either of them had pictured it. For a few minutes, he'd talked back and forth with the girl tending the bar. She'd been more than willing to…entertain him.

But his thoughts had disgusted him. He'd slapped his money on the counter and walked out. That was the night he realized how much the job had changed him, the night he took his last drink of anything stronger than black coffee. He'd headed for home determined to fix his marriage, only to find out he was already too late.

He stared at his truck across the parking lot, eyes squinting against the glare off the windshield. What if he'd treated her better instead of letting his arrogance steal her dignity? Then she might have believed he'd never hurt her the way she thought he had. Then again, what if she'd stood by him and fought for their marriage instead of throwing divorce papers at his head?

He ran a hand down his face. Married when they were barely out of high school. They'd gone through basic training at the same time in different states. Her training overlapped his. Her deployments. His missions. The longer they lived separate lives in the army, the more the gulf between their personal lives widened. It was no wonder she quit on him. They'd gone from best friends with big dreams to strangers sharing a last name and a series of rapidly deteriorating stolen moments.

Now, here he was, ten years later, trapped between mistakes both real and perceived, attempting to win the trust of a woman he was pretty sure never wanted to see him again. But with the threats he'd heard hanging over her head, it was up to him to make sure she lived to see tomorrow.

SIX

Cassidy killed the engine on her Trailblazer and watched the garage door close behind her, her eyes focused on Shane's truck parked to the side of the driveway. Annoyance flickered through her at the comfort she'd felt when she rounded the corner and saw he was still here. Her laptop bag dragged across the console. It was only because she knew someone was in the house, someone who wouldn't try to come after her with a knife.

Her spine shuddered under the weight of what might have been if Shane hadn't been there on Friday to confront the intruder. The image of walking into the house alone, the power out, totally unprepared for a random blow refused to be beaten back. Would she even be breathing right now if it weren't for him?

The thought barely had time to come together before the door to the house opened and Shane stepped into the space, his broad shoulders strong enough to protect her from anything that came after her.

For several breaths, their eyes locked through her windshield.

He was the first to look away.

This was too intimate. It had been years since anyone met her at the door when she came home from work, and the last—the only—person to do it then had been Shane. It was like the previous years folded over on themselves to merge the past and the present in some sort of freakish warp of what was and what might have been.

Cassidy shook her head and curled her lip. No. Forget what might have been. Their marriage was what never should be. Shaking off her traitorous emotions, she shoved her car door open, shouldered her laptop bag and brushed past Shane into the house, ignoring the rush of contact between them. "Did you find anything?"

Silence. She looked up to find Shane standing in the same spot, hand still on the doorknob, eyes focused on the garage.

"Shane?"

It was like he came back from far away, and when his eyes finally swung to her, she knew his thoughts had trekked back through time with hers.

He shook his head as if to clear the ghosts of the past. "What?"

"Did you find anything? On my computer?" She slid her laptop bag onto the counter and dropped her beret on top of it, determined to bring this twisted relationship of convenience back into the present. "Anything that would merit breaking and entering?"

Shane pressed his lips together and shook his head, crossing his arms over a black T-shirt that rode just right across his shoulders. He must have stopped at his place to change before he came here. Cassidy wished he hadn't. His ACUs didn't highlight his muscles quite the way a T-shirt and jeans did. She fervently hoped he hadn't done this on purpose.

"I didn't find anything. I mean, I didn't snoop too hard, but from glancing at file names, all you've got is your personal stuff on there. Web browser, word processor, random files... I have no idea."

She nodded. The air in the room was hard to breathe, thick with the tension of words unspoken. If their lives hadn't diverged, they would have spent most days after work catching up in the kitchen like this, though hopefully not talking about hacked computers and possible terrorists.

Shane finally shut the door and stepped into the room.

His closer proximity jangled her nerves, and she reached down to pull out the salvation of this conversation. "I brought something home with me." With a flourish, she yanked out a palm-sized external drive. "I usually back work stuff up on it, but it's got enough gigs to hold the entire contents of my hard drive."

Shane nodded, his shoulders losing some of their

tension. "Nice. That way if anybody tampers with it when you're not here…"

"I'll know if they took something off."

"Or put something on."

Cassidy knit her eyebrows together. "Why would someone put something on?"

"I'm just saying. We've got no idea what's up, so you never know. Off or on… Either way, you'll know."

"True." She fidgeted with the strap on her laptop bag as the conversation died another agonizing death.

"That your laptop?"

"My personal one. I locked up the government one at work. It would be a lot harder for someone to get to it where I put it than it would be if I left it here tonight."

"Want me to check it out?"

"No. It wasn't here this weekend or when the house got broken into. I let Jackson borrow it."

At her words, Shane's eyebrows drew together in a deep V.

Cassidy's nerves leaped to attention. "What?"

"Nothing." Shane pulled his cell phone from his pocket and dropped it on the counter, then slid her borrowed house key out and held it up, studying it in the light.

"Spill it, Logan." She glanced at the clock on the microwave. Jackson would be here in half an hour.

He tossed the key into the air and caught it, then let it clank to the counter, clearly weighing his attitude and his words. Finally, he took a deep breath. "How well do you know him?"

"I'm sorry?" Exactly what was he getting at? "How is that your business?" As her mind caught up with Shane's obvious train of thought, her anger simmered to the surface. "Are you implying that you suspect him of something? Based on what exactly?"

"Hear me out, Cassy. Right now, I suspect everyone in your life. There's probably no reason for me to, but—"

"You're right. You have no reason. No reason other than you can't stand the thought of my being happy with someone else." Not that she was contemplating a future happiness with Jackson, but still…

Shane's jaw tightened. "Is it really going to come back to that? Maybe we're not what we used to be. Maybe we'll never be there again. But that doesn't mean I won't try to protect you. I'm not rehashing this again. Somebody is planning to make you the fall guy, maybe even kill you if it serves their purposes. I'll suspect anybody in your life that I want until they give me a reason not to."

"Fine." Cassidy felt like a three-year-old in full snit as she snatched her laptop bag and jerked it onto her shoulder. "How about I suspect you? Seems like nothing at all was going on until you showed up."

"Do what you have to do." The level calm of his

voice in the face of her ire only amped up the heat. "But I'm watching the house tonight while you're gone to wherever it is you're going."

"Do what you have to do," she echoed, then reached past him and snatched her key from the counter. "Just stay out of here and leave when I get home."

Shane nodded, lips pressed tightly together, eyeing her as though he wanted to throw one more punch. With a deep breath, he straightened and stalked across the kitchen into the living room. The door slammed so hard behind him that the windows rattled.

The cab of the truck grew warmer by the minute. No breeze whispered through the cracked windows, and Shane didn't dare risk starting the engine to get a little comfort from the air conditioner. If anybody was watching Cassy's house, he didn't want to spook them into hiding.

He reached across the seat and felt for a bottle of water. His eyes never left the white house down the street. If he could just see the front yard and the backyard at the same time...

Shane's grip on the bottle tightened and crackled the sound of crushed plastic through the truck. *God, I can't see it all. I can't do this on my own. There's too much in motion, too many targets on her. You've got to help or—*

A shadow moved across the corner of the lawn. He tossed the bottle aside and leaned forward, arms crossed over the steering wheel. Yep. Someone was edging along the bushes by the driveway. They paused at the side door to the garage, then disappeared inside.

He sat back and gripped the steering wheel until his knuckles ached. As much as jealousy would like him to believe Jackson was the one harassing Cassy, he knew the man couldn't be in two places at once.

His stomach burned. No. Jackson was out somewhere with Cassy right now, probably wining and dining and winning her heart. He couldn't be the one skulking around Cassy's garage.

Swallowing hard, Shane willed away the image of Cassy sharing dinner with another man. It didn't matter one way or the other to him anyway. Once this whole mess was straightened out and she was safe, he'd go his own way again. Even as he thought it, a mental protest roared in to deafen common sense. *Help me let this go so I can help her and move on.*

He forced rebellious thoughts aside and reached for the cell phone in his pocket. Whether Cassy liked it or not, it was time for the police to get involved.

"No." The groan echoed off the windows of the truck. The memory came to him in cinema slow-motion and he could almost watch himself pull his cell from his pocket and slide it onto her kitchen counter. In the heat of his anger this afternoon, he'd left it lying there, useless to him now.

He pounded the steering wheel with his fist and glanced up the street. This was impossible. If he left his post to use another phone, the guy could leave… Or someone else could show up. If he stayed and watched, the police wouldn't get here in time, but at least he'd know if the intruder left the house before Cassy got home. He could kick himself for his stupidity in not thinking this whole watch-the-house plan through.

Shane slumped but kept his eyes on the garage door, foot bouncing a rhythm on the floormat. If the shadowy figure didn't leave the house before Cassy came home, he'd bust in there and haul the guy out on his own with no backup.

Time passed in an agony of tense muscles and second guesses, but it was less than ten minutes before the dark form eased out of the house and slipped across the neighbor's yard, creeping away from Shane.

Now what? He could stay and keep an eye on the house to make sure no one else went in, but the guy would get away. He could take off in pursuit, but there was no telling what could happen while he was gone. The very idea made his arm pulse under the bandage. He'd already endured one round of battlefield medicine. There was no way he wanted to be the recipient of another. *God, help.* It was the best his desperate mind could utter.

Before he could form a plan, a dark sedan slowed and pulled into the driveway.

Shane slid forward in the seat. He glanced at the clock. A little before eight. Short dinner. The corner of his mouth tipped up. This would be a good thing. He well remembered how Cassy could talk when she got going.

His smile of triumph was short-lived. Jackson got out of the car and followed Cassy to the front steps.

Don't let him in. Don't let him in. If they went inside, his mind would never give him rest from the images that would plague him.

He wanted to look away. He couldn't watch her if she decided to kiss another man. There was no way he'd survive. His breaths were ragged.

Shane pressed his back against the seat but sat up almost as quickly. It shouldn't bother him, but his heart couldn't deny it did. It wasn't possible, but the fist clenching in his gut said it was true. He was still in love with Cassy.

And she had moved on to put a new life together with someone else. A life his conscience wouldn't let him interfere with.

Before the thought had time to fully process, movement at the house caught his attention. After a short conversation that included nothing more than a brief hug, Cassy smiled, waved at Jackson and shut the door between them.

In the same instant Shane started to gloat, his fight response shot heat to his muscles. Jackson stepped into the middle of the yard and stared in the direction the trespasser had gone. He flipped his hand into the air before he turned and went to his car.

From the shadows of the neighbor's yard, a dark figure mirrored the gesture, then strode off in the opposite direction.

Cassidy clicked the dead bolt into place, dropped her purse by the door and dashed up the stairs. Her mind whirled like a carnival ride that rotated one way while its cars spun another.

She had seen the gleam in Jackson's eye at the door, the one that said he'd actually considered kissing her good-night. For the first time in the year they'd been friends, he looked at her in a way that made her wonder how much longer this would last. He was her friend, and she trusted him…to a point. If this sudden interest didn't fizzle soon, she hated to think what might happen. It wasn't that he was expendable. More like he couldn't become indispensable. The one guarantee she could give was it wouldn't be her heart that got broken because she wouldn't let it be. God had let Shane crush her heart before, had let soldiers die in front of her eyes, had refused to save her father… There was no way she could survive any more pain.

Tilting the other direction, her mind twisted to the files on her computer. All she wanted was to dig through her hard drive and root out anything that would give her a clue as to why someone would be after her computer. But the instant her foot landed on the carpet of her office, she stopped. The air felt changed, disturbed like an invisible hand had swirled through the room.

Chills ran along her arms and into the top of her head. She should have armed herself and checked the house before she headed for the computer. She should have allowed Shane to stay and not been so determined to one-up him. Somebody had been here, and now she had no way of knowing if they lurked in another room.

Pride. Her stubborn pride was going to get her killed.

Certain she was delusional, she shut the office door and locked it behind her. It would buy her time if unexpected company tried to barge in.

She headed for her desk chair but stopped. That was the problem. Her chair wasn't where she'd left it after she backed up her computer earlier. It rested against the closet door, like someone had needed space…

Space to get under her desk.

"No." She ground her teeth together and knelt to

survey the damage. The computer looked normal. No wires straggled out. No components lay ripped from their housings.

Cassidy sighed, relief bathing her in warmth. She was paranoid. Drug smugglers and exploding cars were playing with her instincts.

A dull gleam bounced from the carpet beside the computer as she moved to scoot from under the desk. Fingers trembling, Cassidy picked up a screw. *It's just a screw. Nothing to get freaked out over.* Her gaze roamed the floor around the computer, searching for anything out of place. Maybe it had simply jarred loose and she hadn't noticed. Maybe—

Fresh streaks marred the dust on top of the machine. Her fingers gripped the screw so tightly it bit into her flesh. Someone had tampered with her computer. Tonight. While she'd been eating pasta and laughing at Jackson's crazy stories.

She rested on her heels and fought rising panic. The house expanded around her, grew too large, provided too many places to hide. Eyes peered through every opening, even the power outlets. She had to get out of here, had to run, before—

A crash and a muffled curse from the hallway slammed against her taut nerves.

A scream forced it's way out of her throat. She fell backward and scrambled away from the office door, cracking her head on the windowsill.

She knew it, knew she should have checked the

house. Knew she shouldn't have left it to Shane to be able to see everything from his hiding place up the street.

Shane. Where was he? With trembling fingers, she fumbled for her cell phone, then balled her fists, remembering too late it lay in her purse at the base of the stairs. For the first time, she wished she hadn't been too cheap to put a landline in the house. Now she'd have to go it alone.

Cassidy glanced around the room. There had to be something she could turn into a weapon. Her gaze landed on the closet. The wood paddles from her grandfather's old canoe were stored against the back corner. She edged to the door and peeked inside, spotting the paddles in the corner. Whoever was prowling around would be picking splinters from their scalp for a long time to come.

Grasping one of the paddles, Cassidy killed the lights and let her eyes adjust to the darkness. The noise stopped, and no other sounds leaked through the bedroom door. Her lungs ached from holding her breath. *Please don't let them be right outside.*

Taking a deep breath, she squeezed her eyes shut and reached for the doorknob, instinct taking over fear.

Pounding assaulted her ears.

Cassidy's calm shattered as the boat paddle thumped to the floor, glancing off her foot.

The sound echoed through the house, rhythmic, insistent. Someone was beating on the kitchen door.

From the hall, a thump, a shuffle, then pounding feet headed for the stairs.

Forgetting any sense of caution, Cassidy flung the door open and took off in pursuit as a shadowed figure hurtled down the stairs. At the front door, Cassidy stretched and caught the fabric of a T-shirt in her fist, slamming her full weight against the intruder. As she did, her foot caught on the doormat.

It was just enough hesitation to destroy her advantage. An elbow to the temple knocked the world off balance. The shadowed figure shoved hard, throwing her against the stairs. Before Cassidy could shake the ringing stars from her head, the front door opened and the person was gone.

SEVEN

Shane balled his fist and pounded against the door. If Cassy didn't answer in three seconds, he would—

He stumbled as his hand met empty air. His upper body followed the force of his swing toward the door that was no longer there.

Cassy stood just out of reach in the semidark kitchen. "Where were you?" The words trembled low, but they carried the force of a shout.

Shane tried to square his shoulders, but the sight of her stunned him. The emotions he'd allowed himself to acknowledge less than half an hour before were too raw to be in her presence. He should leave, before he spilled everything and she slammed the door in his face.

The revelation forced him to reevaluate the need to share his suspicions about Jackson. If he forced his way into the kitchen and tried to tell her the man she'd been on a date with was also the man responsible for the break-in at her house, she'd write it off as jealousy. He clenched his jaw and felt as though he were sliding off a mountain and couldn't get a handhold to slow his descent. *God, help me handle this the right way.*

His gaze swept over her. She usually took care to stand in a posture of authority. The silhouette of slumped shoulders and half-bowed head tripped his sensors. This was not the same woman he saw on the porch a few minutes ago. "Cassy? Talk to me."

"I—" She wavered and grasped the door handle tighter. As she did, her face fell into the reflected glow of the neighbor's floodlights. She was scared. He could read it in the intensity of her eyes. They were darker than usual, almost bottomless. An angry welt across her upper cheek shifted into the light.

Shane sucked in air and gripped the door frame to steady himself, stopping just short of pulling her to him. As much as he wanted to wrap his arms around her and protect her, this was something he'd have to take slow. "What happened?" If Jackson had somehow managed to lay a hand on her and Shane had missed it… He'd never forgive himself and wouldn't answer for what happened to the other man.

"They got away."

The words took a second to penetrate the anger fogging Shane's reason. "What? Who's 'they'?"

"There was a person… They ran out the front door when you knocked on the back door." Her hand drifted to her face and fingered the darkening bruise. "I almost had them."

Realization left Shane feeling like a green recruit who'd blown his first tactics test. "The guy… He was a distraction."

Cassidy's head jerked up. She winced against the motion. "What guy?"

Punctured by anger, Shane's confidence deflated. "The guy who broke into your garage. I was all eyes on him. They knew I was watching. As long as I was focused on him, someone else could come in the back." He pounded his fist against the door frame, the sharp edge of the wood driving a jolt up his nerves. "I knew I had a bad position, but I kept it. Stupid." Regret pounding along with the pain in his fist, he reached for her shoulder. "Cassy, I'm sorry. I—I could have gotten you killed."

She backed away, out of his reach. "Don't. Don't touch me right now."

"Okay." Shane held both hands up in acquiescence. What could he have done to make her say that now of all times? Unless she was afraid she was too weak to fight something she was feeling….

No. There was no way she'd go there, especially now. And he should be ashamed of himself for even thinking of his emotions when she was obviously in pain. "Can I at least come in and take a look at your face?"

She tensed and started to shake her head.

Shane jumped to his psychological training. Keep her talking. Don't give her the chance to say no.

"Did they mess with anything in here?" He edged his foot closer to the door.

Her shoulders slumped. "Just the computer. I was interrupted before I could power it up and find out if it works."

"The computer? Again?"

"Well…" Cassy stared into the yard behind him, and he knew she was placing her words on a balance. After what felt like an eternity, she sighed and pulled the door open wider. "You might as well come in. I know you're going to keep pushing until you're convinced I'm really okay."

He swallowed the slight smile that tried to surface. It ought to scare him that she'd seen through him that easily. He tipped his head toward the kitchen table. "Is it okay if I sit?"

Cassy nodded and shut the door, flipped on the lights, then edged around the table to close the blinds. She prowled the room like she expected someone to jump out of the closet and yell *boo*.

He couldn't fault her for that particular fear. It probably started with his appearance on Friday, and this little incident tonight hadn't helped. "I'm sorry about the closet thing."

She yanked the refrigerator door open and shrugged. "That's the least of my worries. Want anything to drink?"

"You have lemonade?" Barring any truly bizarre changes in her life over the past few years, he knew there would be lemonade. It was part of her makeup, a quirk she'd picked up from her mother and carried forward as some ritual sense of stability after her father died. After her first tour in Iraq, she'd consumed gallons of it until she'd nearly destroyed her stomach.

He watched her pull the pitcher from the fridge and move to the counter. Every move seemed timed. Her threat level sat firmly on red, and he had no idea how to bring it down. "Tell me about the computer."

Bringing the pitcher with her, she sat down across from him and slid a glass across the table. "It's definitely been tampered with. They probably didn't know I'd backed it up before they got in here tonight."

Shane eased out of the chair and went to the freezer. It was almost bare, but he found what he needed and came back to the table, dropping a bag of frozen vegetables in front of her. "If you won't let me look at it, at least put that on it. Your soldiers are going to think you got into a wicked fist fight tomorrow."

She sniffed a short laugh but obeyed, holding the package against her temple, wincing as cold met pain.

Shane had never before realized it was possible to physically ache with the need to touch someone. There wasn't a muscle in his body that didn't want to shield her, take that fearful look out of her eyes.

She needed to let him handle it, to know he would protect her. He scowled. Yeah, he'd done a bang-up job of that tonight.

He watched her slide her glass in small circles, fear written in the condensation trail on the table. She wouldn't sleep tonight. She'd wander the house, armed with whatever makeshift weapon she could find, waiting for someone to burst through the dining-room window. He couldn't bear to think of her living that way, patrolling her own home like it was a forward operating base and the Taliban were right outside the gates. Cassy had lived on high alert long enough. She deserved some peace on her home turf.

Digging the side of his fist into his thigh, Shane slid back in the chair and tried to project nonchalance, even as he ached and strained to keep her from harm. Maybe if he exuded calm, Cassy would take her cues from him. "You going to call the police?"

Her hand froze on the side of the glass, and she stared at it for a long time before she lifted her eyes. "I don't know. What are they going to do? Take a report and get back to me? You don't have enough evidence yet. And think about how it sounds. 'Gee, Officer, my desk chair was moved and some crazy person I didn't see hit me in the eye. No, it's not a robbery. Oh, and the one person who can corroborate this is the guy I was married to ten years ago. He was staking out my house.' It won't fly." She flicked a glance at him. "Either that or they'll arrest you for stalking or worse."

"Cassy, somebody broke into your house and attacked you. Don't you think you should—"

The table rocked as she slammed her glass down and threw the frozen vegetables to the floor. "You do not get to boss me around. You don't get to come in here and mess with my head and—"

"No." He held his palm up and, miraculously, she didn't finish her sentence. "I get it. I get you're mad. I get you're over me." His mouth refused to form new words until a fresh wave of emotion passed. "I get that you think I've done something I'd never ever do. And deep down, you know I wouldn't, no matter what any evidence tells you."

Cassy moved to speak, but the look Shane gave her was hard enough to stem her words. "What happened tonight has nothing to do with that. Right now, this minute, at this table, I'm the only person you can trust. And whether we're together or not, we have a history, and I will still do all I can to protect you. Once you get that through your head, we'll be doing a lot better." He sat back and waited to see what sort of response his stand would evoke.

It took about three seconds for the bomb to go off. Both of Cassy's palms crashed into the table, and she stood so quickly her chair teetered on the edge of a backflip. "Well, you failed as a husband,

and you failed to protect me tonight, didn't you?"
She balled her fists.

Shane tensed. No physical punch could hurt as
badly as the verbal one she'd just thrown. The pain
landed square at the center of his chest, where the
guilt still lodged. Where they'd once been each other's everything, shared their dreams of saving the
world together, now they stood on opposite sides
of the same canyon, fighting for the same goal, but
unable to reach each other across the distance. But
while it was true there were times he'd utterly disrespected her, he'd never been able to puzzle out
what finally set her off, why she chose to pitch divorce papers at him and slam the door in his face…
just as he'd been ready to make good on his promise to honor her.

Instead of swinging, Cassy snatched her lemonade glass and stalked to the sink. She dumped the
contents and stood staring down after them. "And as
for trusting you…" The words wobbled. "My head
does, but my heart just can't."

Silence seeped into the kitchen behind her out-
burst. It thickened the air and made it hard for Shane
to catch his breath. For the first time, he saw beneath
Cassy's anger, and his neck burned. He'd spent a
long time staring into his own pain and dealing with
her fury, but he'd never really understood the magnitude of what his arrogance had done to the woman
he'd loved…to the woman he still loved. Only the

fact she'd faced physical danger tonight let her emotions spill out now.

The ragged edges of a choked sob ripped at his heart and drew his eyes to her. Shane knew he shouldn't touch her, was certain it would only provoke her further, but he couldn't stop his legs from standing, couldn't keep his feet from crossing the room, couldn't prevent his arms from wrapping around her waist.

She stiffened and sucked in a quick breath as he laid his cheek against the back of her head. "I am so sorry you're going through this, Cassy. I wish I had been smarter tonight and seen what they were up to. I should have been here."

For the briefest moment, she hesitated, then leaned back against his chest, sweeping gusts of bittersweet emotion across his skin. "You couldn't have known they'd figure us out."

"I tried not to be seen around the house. That's why I came to the back door instead of the front tonight, but I guess, somehow…" The words tripped over the raw edges of his heart. Stupid. The rigger shed. He'd gone to her unit twice and been seen by half of the people there. And he'd stormed out her front door this afternoon. Yet another thing he hadn't thought through. She was like a vortex that sucked in his common sense and whirled out emotion. Shane took a step back, craving distance to clear the fog she swept into his reason.

There was a slight instant of hesitation before Cassy turned to lean against the counter, crossing her arms over her chest, building a barrier between them. "I know what you're thinking. It's definitely some of my soldiers. How else would anyone know you're looking around?"

"It's the only explanation I've got."

"Did you get a good look at the guy?"

"No, but he was still in the neighbor's yard when you got home." He stopped the story right there. If he mentioned his suspicions about Jackson, she was likely to build an even taller wall between them. All he had to go on when it came to the man was a hand motion and a gut feeling. A gut feeling that could be nothing more than jade-green jealousy.

"He was next door? When I got home?" Cassy gripped her arms tighter around her stomach, but Shane still saw her shudder. "So there were two of them waiting for me."

He knew then that he couldn't leave her alone. "I'm staying."

"What?"

"No matter what you think about me or what you think about the situation, you can't stay here alone. If you're not going to call the police, then you're going to deal with me being here to keep an eye out. I'll sleep in the trailer, if you don't want me in the house. But if you tell me no, I'll camp out on the front porch for the whole world to see." He waited for her to look up, but she didn't move. "It's your call."

Rain pounded the roof as wind blasted it against the house in a full frontal assault. Cassidy pulled the edge of the blinds away from the window and tried to see the backyard, but the water running in rivers down the window blocked her view. Lightning sliced the sky, and she jumped backward, dropping the blinds as thunder cracked overhead.

She sank to the edge of the bed and stared at the floor. This vulnerable feeling made her weak. And she hated weakness, especially her own.

Shane patrolled downstairs, checking door locks and testing window latches. The soft sounds of his movements filtered up the stairs, and she followed every step with her ears as he moved from the kitchen through the dining room and into the den.

Patterns formed in the carpet beneath her circling toe, and she drew in a deep breath, holding it until her sore temple pounded and her lungs forced her to exhale. There was something about Shane that filled every inch of the air around him, that took over the oxygen until it felt like she was breathing him in. He demanded attention. And the longer he was around, the more her attention turned toward him. This could get even more dangerous than drug smugglers and death threats.

Her toe stopped its circling. It's what had drawn

her to him in the first place, the way he strode into their lit class the first day of their freshman year, like he owned the place but without arrogance, like he wanted to make everybody feel like they belonged. He'd sat behind her and hadn't said a word for three weeks, but she'd been deeply aware of every breath he took. It was years later before he told her he'd been scared silent by the thought of making a fool of himself in front of her.

She smiled in spite of her circumstances. It was hard to believe a man with Shane's confidence had been unable to work up the nerve to speak once he was near her. But it's what he'd always said, and she'd had no reason to doubt him.

Cassidy dug her toes into the carpet and gripped the side of the mattress. He'd probably used the same line dozens of times on who knew how many other girls.

With Shane, life had soared. Once he finally spoke to her, they were inseparable, best friends. "Army brats" of soldier fathers, both of them had grown up knowing their duty lay in continuing their families' service, in doing something to give back. He'd always wanted to be in Special Forces. Her head for organization and drive to serve others had steered her toward support.

Then, in their senior year, everything about that friendship changed when they both suddenly realized they didn't want to live without each other. He'd been her confidant through every trial, had held her on the nights when Iraq came screaming into her sleep after her first tour.

The lump lodged in her throat with a dagger's edge, but she managed to swallow it, to quell the shaking before it could start. This wasn't the time for those tears.

It took effort to drag her thoughts back into line. Everything had been amazing, until Shane went Special Forces and that confident stride mutated into an arrogant swagger. Living nightmares from her first round in Iraq and her father's illness threw Cassidy into a freefall away from God at the same time Shane spiraled into habits he'd promised he'd never pick up.

Their landing had been like a leap without a parachute, the whole relationship burning in on a screaming malfunction. Too young, too much time apart, too many temptations...

A creak on the stairs snapped her thoughts in two. Her entire body tensed with the memory of the last sound she'd heard in the hall. Her muscles grew tighter with the realization that it was Shane at the top of the landing, not twenty feet away. She steeled herself for battle, not against Shane, but against the part of her heart that wanted to forget what had happened, to scrub the memories from her brain and to make everything between them right again. The same part of her that had leaned into him for support tonight… Until he stepped away and took another small piece of her with him.

It was impossible. There was no way he could turn back the calendar and erase what he'd done to her. She'd let him play protector, but she couldn't let him back in her heart. That was a pain she couldn't afford.

She sucked her lower lip between her teeth. Shane thought she wouldn't sleep tonight unless he was here. But in reality she wouldn't sleep tonight *because* he was here. There was physical safety with him nearby, but the danger to her emotions was undeniable.

The stairs creaked, then the front door shut. Cassidy tiptoed to her bedroom door to peek down the hall, missing a step as thunder rolled over the house again. He hadn't even said good-night. She tipped her chin and stood straighter. It didn't matter. Her heart didn't need his attention, didn't want his affection, didn't need to keep imagining how it would feel if they could turn the clock back and start over again.

Footprints dented the carpet along the hall, his steps mixed with hers, the way it used to be. Her hand went to her stomach, covering the hollow place that expanded with each passing second. It could be heartburn, worry, exhaustion… Anything but a longing for what used to be. She drew her eyebrows together. The only person in the world she could depend on was herself. God had taught her that when He'd refused to provide safety, when He'd ignored her desperate cries and taken her father. Shane had taught her that when he destroyed her trust. It was something she could not, should not, ever forget. If only—

Shane cleared his throat, and Cassidy jumped, reaching behind her to grip the wall. He'd come back into the house and stood halfway up the stairs, watching her with an unreadable expression. She didn't know how long he'd stood there while she was lost in what should have been.

"I just..." Shane gestured toward her, then dropped his hand to his side. "I wanted to tell you..." He cleared his throat again, glanced at the floor, then looked up and captured her gaze. "Promise me you'll stay in your room and lock the door."

She nodded. *That's all?*

"Okay." He gave a half wave, his eyes locked on hers. "Good night, Cassy."

The lump that formed in Cassidy's throat blocked the pulses her brain tried to send to her muscles. She stood frozen, trapped by his green eyes, unable to move past this moment and this thing that zipped between them. It was like the storm outside had blasted lightning through the roof, and the volts rocketed between them.

Thunder ripped through the house and left its imprint on her eardrums as the lights flickered off, then on again. Cassidy pressed her back into the wood behind her, and the energy between Shane and her vanished with the echo of the thunder.

She swallowed hard. "Good night." Without waiting for Shane's response, she slipped into the bedroom and shut the door, then stared at the handle. After hesitating, she twisted the lock, then studied the dresser, wondering how hard it would be to move it and further seal the entrance.

But would it be to keep danger out? Or to keep her from going to Shane to beg him for another chance?

EIGHT

The numbers on Shane's watch glowed bright in the darkness of the camper: 2:37. He dropped his hand and rolled over onto his side, fixing his eyes on the awning windows. He'd cracked them open to let storm-cooled air in after the rain stopped, and a soft glow from the streetlights filtered in. Because sleep refused to come, he'd wandered around the outside of the house through the damp grass every thirty minutes, ears attuned to anything out of the ordinary, anything to indicate someone was trying to find a way in.

And he'd prayed harder than he ever had in his life. It had been one thing for him to confront an assailant in her kitchen, but another thing entirely to know she'd faced the brunt of an attack.

When he left the house after saying good-night to Cassy, he'd detoured through the garage to cool down and to check the side door for signs of forced entry. None. Whoever was coming and going was either a professional or they had a key. A key Jackson himself could have handed the guy. Indecision worse than any hunger gnawed at his gut. He should have told Cassy what he'd seen, should have found a way to make her understand. But what if he'd misinterpreted everything? Jackson could have thought that the shadowy figure was a neighbor. If Shane went to Cassy with an accusation that proved false, it would sever the tenuous thread of her trust.

Shane flipped onto his back and looked for a cool spot in the sheets. Here he'd worried Cassy would suffer from a sleepless night. Instead, he was the one who still chased rest. For the past few hours his thoughts had bounced between the situation and gut-deep prayer. God either had to change his feelings or take him far away from here. There was no way he could live and work in the same town as Cassy and keep his sanity. The problem was there wasn't any place on the planet far enough to erase his thoughts.

His body snapped into high alert every time the trees creaked in the wind, but he couldn't decide if it was the fear of someone skulking around the house or the hope of Cassy coming to talk this whole thing out once and for all. Wonder what she'd do if she realized it would only take one spoken word to make him hers forever? He curled his lip and folded his hands behind his head. Yeah. It was more likely he'd have to fight off an intruder than get a reconciliatory gesture out of her. Not a lot of men in the world could make claims like those. Most guys in the world were luckier than he was.

A muted scrape forced him straight up in the bed. The covers tumbled to his waist. His pulse pounded against his veins as he strained to hear the noise again, but nothing out of the ordinary came to his ears.

Shane untangled his hands from the covers and hit the button on his watch: 4:29. He'd fallen asleep. In the past he'd have cursed enough to peel the paint from the walls, but now the words burned his throat as he swallowed them.

Tense shoulder muscles pulled taut as he stretched his arms over his head. Well, he was awake. Might as well make a circuit of the house again, just to be sure. Shane slipped on his running shoes and yanked open the door, his focus on the front of the house.

Movement flickered as the blinds in the dining room dropped into place and a light passed the window. His foot froze halfway between the metal trailer step and the ground. Someone was in the house. His first instinct demanded he rush through the front door and up the stairs to make sure Cassy was okay, but he forced himself to take a deep breath. It could be Cassy…

But she'd promised to stay in her room with the door locked.

Shane dragged his hand across his face and down the front of his neck. He'd need the element of surprise to catch whoever skulked around downstairs. Easing across the yard, he stopped at the front door and pulled out the key Cassy had reluctantly returned to him. He'd have to move slowly to keep from giving away his position.

Years of combat training took control and curbed his emotions as he eased the door open, crept into the living room and listened. No sound. No light. He slipped halfway up the stairs, aiming to make sure Cassy's door was still shut, but stopped. Maybe he'd imagined the whole thing. If that was the case, Cassy would kill him for stepping foot into the house for no good reason.

From this vantage point, he could overlook the den, and he stopped once more to listen. It was too dark to see anything if he looked directly at it. He slid along the wall to the bottom step and relied on peripheral vision to pick up any movement.

An explosion of sound… "Shane!" Cassy's sudden shriek tore at his eardrums and set his feet toward the kitchen before he could spark a thought. *Not again. Not twice in one night.*

His feet hit the kitchen linoleum in a skidding halt, his senses overwhelmed by the sounds of struggle. A thud, a man's mutter…

Shane felt by the door, praying for a light switch. His fingers skipped over the plastic cover and flipped. Light flooded the room, blinding him and drawing a halt to all other noise.

It took only a moment for him to blink reality into focus. The knife-wielding man who'd attacked him had Cassy pinned into a headlock, clearly dragging her for the open door. Scratch marks raked down his face, and blood dripped from a rapidly swelling lip.

His shock at Shane's appearance gave Cassy the advantage. Before Shane could jump in and rescue her, she kicked into the same move she'd used on him a few days before, landing her bare heel hard into the guy's instep. Arms loosened enough for her to tuck and roll away, and Shane lunged. He landed one hard blow, but as he reared back for another, the man broke free and bolted out the door.

Shane hesitated, glancing back at Cassy, who cradled her foot on the floor. He couldn't leave her alone now.

Her eyes widened. "Go!"

In the next breath, he took off out the door to the fence gate, but squealing tires at the front of the house told him there had been a car waiting, and he'd hesitated too long.

Shane kicked the gate shut and stalked back to the house, angry at himself for falling asleep, for leaving Cassy to fight for herself, for second-guessing himself. He stepped back into the kitchen in a fog of self-recrimination.

Cassy was gone.

The soft sound of the front door slipping shut

added speed to his step, and he found Cassy, forehead pressed against the door, breaths ragged.

He touched her shoulder, and she whirled, prepared to fight, panic driving her blows.

Shane pulled her tight against him. "Cassy, it's me." She fought harder. "It's me. I've got you." Shane pitched his voice low, trying to puncture the fear and adrenaline that drove her.

She landed an elbow to his stomach, dropped to the floor and scrambled away before she stopped struggling. "Shane?" The word floated on the edge of tears.

Shane slid to the side and leaned against the wall, struggling to catch his breath as Cassy fought back sobs he knew she'd never release to the open air. He weighed his options before he inched along the wall toward her. Slipping his arms around her, he pulled her into his lap and cradled her against his chest, not wanting to note how right she felt, like she'd never been anywhere else. "I'm so sorry." His whisper rasped against the top of her head as the crisp citrus of her shampoo tickled his senses. "I fell asleep and I let them get in. And then…I didn't mean to scare—"

"I thought you were them." Cassy's words were ragged. She melted against him, gripping his arms like he was the only solid thing in her world.

The wall Shane had tried to build around his heart crumbled as she clung to him. He wanted to keep her at arm's length, wanted to let her go the way she'd let him go, but she was so soft in his arms, so scared, so…needing him. His breathing was too shallow, his thinking too fogged as the fight response in him faded and he grew more aware of the relief that seeped in at her safety, of the love he still felt for the woman in his arms where she belonged.

Cassy's breathing slowed, but she didn't pull away from him. She stayed, resting against him as the panic subsided.

"Did he hurt you?"

She shook her head against his chest. "I'm good. Just need a minute."

"Why were you downstairs?" His arms tightened around her. "I told you to stay in your room with the door locked."

"I thought I heard you come in."

Shane cleared his throat and fought to clear his head at the same time. "You called me."

"What?"

"Just now. In the kitchen. You called for me." It wasn't what he'd set out to say, but the idea she'd needed him overrode everything else.

The silence stretched out long and unbroken. She tilted her head. "I knew you'd come." The breath of her words brushed against his cheek and shot warmth to his frazzled nerves. It would only take a tilt of his head—

Before he could finish the thought, her arms were around his neck and her lips were on his.

For the first time in almost a decade, Cassidy felt like she was truly home. Here, in the midst of chaos, was safety.

Shane stiffened in her embrace, then pulled her closer and returned the kiss. Something in his posture had shifted as he held her, had softened and taken her in, driving her to connect.

It felt as though she'd been falling through a bottomless pit, and she couldn't remember when the descent began. She only knew that here and now, Shane had caught her. This kiss calmed her, grounded her to the one place in the world that was safe…

Until she remembered Shane was the very person who'd pushed her off the ledge to begin with.

Cassidy untangled herself from Shane's arms. The room spun around her as she skittered away and pulled her knees to her chest.

"Cassy."

"No." She held out her palms, even though she knew he couldn't see her in the darkness. Harsh cold cracked her heart and seeped outward into her fingertips. Cassidy shivered and wrapped her arms around her knees. Her safety was gone, security shattered. There was nowhere to run when the world got crazy because the insanity began and ended with the man in front of her.

Shane didn't move.

When she felt like her nerves would implode from the silence, she broke it. "You're not going to defend yourself this time?"

"You were just attacked in your own house. Now is not the time. You're projecting."

"Projecting?"

"Throwing your fear about what just happened onto me." He stood and looked down at her. "They're gone. Whoever they are, they're gone. And we'll get to the—"

"You're right." She squared her shoulders and fought down rising panic at the thought of where she could be right now if Shane hadn't stepped in. Again. Why was it he was always there right when she needed him?

No, she didn't need him. She could take care of herself. Her training, her experiences, her life… It had all prepared her to defend herself. And she could do it. She didn't need Shane, and she definitely didn't need what had just happened between them.

"Can I ask you a question?" Shane's voice came to her from the semidarkness.

She stiffened, terrified of questions she didn't know how to answer. Her heart begged her to forgive him, to let him protect her. But her mind wouldn't let her. *You can never trust him. Never. He's let you down before. He'll do it again and again.*

"What do you trust, Cassy?"

The question slapped her across the cheek. Nothing. There was nothing in the world worthy of her trust. She flinched and swallowed hard, slipping up to sit on the edge of the coffee table. "Me."

"What happened to God?"

Her prepared denials stuck in her throat at the turn she'd never expected. The conversational shift forced her brain to blaze a new path. "God? Really? Since when is God important to you? I seem to remember you and Him weren't exactly on speaking terms. And after all He's let happen to me, it's pretty clear I'm better off on my own."

"Cassy—"

"Don't. I begged Him, Shane. Begged Him. Begged Him to bring us all back from Iraq. He didn't. You know what it's like to see them die, right in front of you. Don't pretend you don't. Where is He in that?"

"You can't—"

"No. He can't. Or He won't. And then," her voice grew ragged as it rose higher, and she had to swallow hard to keep the pain from pouring out, "I came home. And you… And Dad. I begged, Shane. I begged. And He didn't care. It doesn't matter how much you pray. It doesn't matter how much faith you have or how much you want it. None of it matters. It can't be fixed. I don't need His help. I can make a big enough mess right by myself."

Shane exhaled in a way that spoke of wasted defeat. "I'm sorry to hear that." Shoulders slumped, he walked to the front door.

Panic gripped her so hard that she shook from the inside out. "Wait." She hated the way her voice cracked, but she couldn't be alone. Not now. What if those people— "Where are you going?"

Shane stopped, one foot on the front porch and one on the hardwood of the entryway. One half in her life, one half out. "To get my cell phone out of the trailer. This has gone far enough. I'm calling the police." He vanished into the night.

With Shane gone, there was no distraction to drown out his words. Who did she trust? She should be furious at him for the question, but the anger refused to boil. Instead, loneliness seeped in and wrapped her in a cold embrace.

If only she'd stayed upstairs. She'd have been able to defend herself from up there. Shane wouldn't have had to save her. And maybe she'd be reveling in the triumph over her shadowy enemies instead of re-playing a moment that never should have happened.

Before she could beat herself up any more, Shane reappeared, backlit by the streetlights.

"I'm sorry." The words escaped her before she could stop them, and she leaned back to flip on the table lamp, wanting to see his reaction.

The glare slapped her eyelids shut and threw a strong dose of reality onto the scene. When her eyes adjusted, Shane was leaning against the front door with his arms crossed over his chest, looking at her like he was afraid she might sprout fangs and bite him.

Cassidy wanted to slink up the stairs and crawl under the covers, never to come out. "Don't look at me that way," she mumbled. "It makes me feel like you expect me to growl like a rabid dog."

His sudden grin sat crooked on his face, and his rumpled hair made him look like a sleepy little boy.

Cassidy dropped her gaze to his feet.

He stepped closer. "I called them. They'll be here in a few minutes."

The nearer he came, the faster her heart beat. It took a moment for her to piece together words that answered his question and didn't involve something she'd regret in the light of day. "Are you going to tell them everything?"

"Not everything, but that someone's broken in here repeatedly. We don't have enough about the drugs to say anything yet. And I'm not sure I want to mention your computer being a target. They'd take it with them before we had a chance to look it over." It seemed he'd forgotten their kiss and had moved on to more practical things. It should have relieved her.

"You're assuming that the processor is still intact."

"You're right. And you could plug the hard drive in and find out the whole system's been wiped clean and programmed to destroy external data, too."

That was one thing Cassidy hadn't considered. Defeat dragged her spirit to the floor. "Great. Everything in my house is suspect. For all I know there are mini cameras and hidden microphones tucked into every crevice, too." She shuddered, her gaze taking in every corner of the room.

"I don't see any reason for that." Shane settled on the coffee table beside her. Cassidy noticed he was careful not to get too close. "Can you trust me to deal with the computer?"

Right now, she couldn't trust herself not to fling her arms around his neck. "I'm going to tell you the truth, Shane. I'm not a hundred percent sure who I trust anymore."

"I know. But I also know somebody who can sniff out any problems with the desktop."

"Who?"

"I've got a buddy, Derek. You met him once or twice." He shifted slightly away from her. "A long time ago."

Cassidy sighed. "Bring him over if you think he can take care of the problem."

The sound of an engine in the driveway halted the conversation. Cassidy wished she felt relief, but all she could sense was bone-jarring exhaustion.

Shane stood and headed for the front door. Hand on the knob, he turned to look back at her. "It will all work out, Cassy. I promise."

NINE

Cassidy rubbed her eyes and leaned back in her desk chair to stare at the tiled ceiling of her office at work. Her body ached, and her mind stood on full guard. What she'd just seen had to be a trick of her sleep-deprived mind and weary eyes. The police had stayed until after dawn. Even if they hadn't, she knew sleep never would have come to her anyway.

Her chair squeaked as she dropped heavily against the back, rubbing her temples with her fingertips. Over the years, she'd survived basic training, Airborne School, the transition from the Enlisted side of the house to the Warrant Officer side and faced combat zones. She'd never felt this weary and disconnected. And she'd certainly never felt like the world was spinning and there was nothing solid to grab on to.

When her head was clear, she picked up the printed copy of the container inventory she'd requested yesterday. Her eyes scanned the pallet numbers and weights. Everything looked to be in order.

The paper slipped to her desk, and she studied her computer screen, where she'd downloaded the copy from her army email account. There it was in black and white. There was no way to deny what her eyes saw.

This morning, Cassidy told Shane they needed more help, and they made the decision to test Mac. With all of her heart she believed he wasn't one of the bad guys, but Shane insisted they be sure. Wanting to see if some of her suspicions were right before calling the older man in, she'd left Shane to chat with her master sergeant while she booted her computer to start her own investigation. Whatever Anderson had done in his two minutes of tinkering had worked. He'd used her ID and clicked right in. She hadn't had a problem since.

After straightening in her chair to take another look at the numbers, she made a decision. This was bigger than her. "Mac?"

"Ma'am?" The master sergeant appeared in the doorway, Shane close at his heels.

She dropped her gaze to her desk and wondered if she'd ever be able to look at him again without remembering last night's kiss.

Cassidy waved them in and motioned for Shane to shut the door. He did, then stayed close to the entrance as though he wanted to be on guard in case Mac didn't respond with the innocence Cassidy hoped for.

McIntyre sat when she gestured to the chair in front of her. When she slid the hard copy of the inventory across her desk, he leaned forward and took it. "This is the inventory for the shipping containers coming in this week. That's not something you'd normally worry yourself with, is it?" No surprise or recognition flickered on Mac's face. That was a good sign.

At the door, Shane relaxed, but just slightly. His shoulders were still turned toward the older man, his body clearly prepared to move if need be. Irrationally, Cassidy hoped Mac wouldn't sneeze. The sudden movement might get him tackled.

"Let's just say there wasn't a lot of sleep to be found in my house last night," she flickered a glance at Shane, "and that's when I remembered something." The word *stupid* had flashed on her brain most of the morning. It was out of bounds for her not to have picked up on this sooner.

"I'm not tracking what you're getting at." Mac tapped the papers against his knee. Every action appeared genuine to Cassidy's probing gaze.

"Take a look at the weights for the pallets we've got coming in from Afghanistan. They have to be accurate so when the loadmaster calculates how to load the aircraft, he can keep everything balanced, right? Anything look off to you on this load?"

He flipped pages, scratching his chin. It was several minutes before he looked up. "I think you're seeing things. Everything looks kosher."

"*There,* on the copy I got, everything's in order." She turned her computer monitor toward him. "This is the copy I downloaded off my email this morning. I've got a buddy working as a Unit Movement Officer in Afghanistan. He emailed me and said the pallets seemed a little off when they loaded them. He figured our guys over there got careless and didn't shake out enough sand. It was too late for them to take a look at what was going on, but he emailed me the weights in case we needed to come down on anybody about not taking care of business."

"Seems reasonable," Shane muttered, but a glance at his face told Cassidy the set of his jaw grew more tense by the moment. Now, Mac's reaction to this would tell them everything.

"I've seen weights off before. A few pounds here and there. Nothing new. Your buddy's right. Usually too much sand in the gear." McIntyre scanned the computer screen for all of three seconds before his head snapped up and his eyes locked on hers. "This is wrong." Disbelief creased lines into his forehead as he turned to the papers in his hand. "I've been around shipments like this my whole career, and these are all way off. Look at this." He jabbed a finger and the pages rattled. "Some of them are right, but some of them are too heavy. They're balanced, so they're safe to ship, but no pallet carrying chutes back ought to weigh so far from the norm, no matter how much debris is in it. Somebody on the front end screwed up big-time." He held the printed inventory next to the computer and compared the two copies. "And these two don't match. This one," he shook the hard copy inventory from the UMO, "looks more like a normal load. What's going on here?"

Cassidy turned her attention to Shane to gauge his reaction. His shoulders eased into a more relaxed posture, and he leaned back against the door.

"We're not sure yet." It wasn't the time to reveal everything, even though relief that Mac appeared innocent mingled with an amped-up sense of urgency over his agreement with what she'd found. They now had concrete proof that something wasn't right, that someone could have used their parachutes as delivery vehicles for any manner of illegal substances. But was it enough? Cassidy feigned a calm she didn't feel. "And here I thought I was crazy from lack of sleep." She turned the monitor toward her. "I want to talk to Anderson. Is he in yet?"

"It's a little early for PT, but anything's possible. You think he might have something to do with this?"

Cassidy sat back and let her eyes rest on the computer screen, random thoughts coming together to form complete pictures. "Hear us out."

"Us?" Mac twisted in his chair to look at Shane, who straightened under the scrutiny. "So I was right? You're here investigating something."

"Not officially." The short words made it clear that was all the answer Shane was going to offer.

The master sergeant turned back to Cassidy. "Tell me what's going on with our soldiers."

She ignored the breach of protocol, knowing he wasn't trying to lay down an order to his superior. "Just follow me here and see if you come to the same conclusion." At his nod, she went on. "I get an email telling me our shipment is screwed up. And the copy I printed is missing."

"Yep."

"The same day, somebody breaks into my house, and I'm pretty sure at this point that it has every-thing to do with my computer. When I come in on Monday, my desktop tells me I've had invalid log in attempts and refuses to let me into the system. Who fixes my desktop?" She leveled her gaze on Mac.

"Anderson."

"And whose car went Fourth of July in the parking lot?" She stopped there. No need to tell him she'd been attacked twice in her own house.

Mac pressed his lips together. "You've got a tenu-ous thread there, especially because that was ruled an accident pretty quickly."

"It's the only thread I've got." A crash from the front office punctuated her words and rammed her heart into overdrive.

Mac jumped to his feet as Shane yanked the door open, prepared to defend as necessary.

Cassidy's pulse pounded against her skin until Shane relaxed and stepped back.

"Chief?" Sergeant Landon ran a glance up and down Shane. For the space of a heartbeat, recognition and something that looked like a flicker of disgust hardened her expression, but it fell away before Cassidy could be sure it was really there. "Sorry. I just dropped every file I had on the new T-11 chutes." Her eyes drifted to Shane again in a way that almost seemed like she was sizing him up as an opponent.

"Did you need something, Sergeant?" Cassidy tapped her booted toe, out of patience and almost out of energy for rational thought.

"Yes, ma'am. We need Master Sergeant McIntyre on the pack floor. One of the new riggers has a question none of us can answer."

"He'll be there shortly."

Landon nodded and backed out, a slight shuffle from the next room the only indication she stuck around long enough to gather her files.

Shane's gaze followed her as though he were trying to piece the woman's behavior into a puzzle. He watched until silence reigned in the office, then shifted his focus back into the room. "She's gone."

"You're thinking something."

A smile flicked at the corner of Shane's lips. "You noticed?" Before Cassidy could respond, all traces of amusement vanished. "How long has that female sergeant been here?"

Cassidy flicked a glace at Mac. "Six months?"

"Seems like she got here right before we went on leave for Christmas." Mac looked into the distance as though he could see a calendar in the air. "Yeah. Seems like she'd just started getting into the groove here and then we went on block leave and she had to start all over again." He focused on Shane. "Why?"

"Ever had somebody's personality just rub you the wrong way?"

"Do you really want me to answer that question?" Cassidy smiled at Shane's fake grimace.

"Probably not."

"That's enough flirting, you two." Mac's amused words sliced the connection between them.

Shane's eyes flicked wider, and he seemed to find the corner of the room above her head fascinating.

Mac turned to Cassidy, who could feel her face growing hotter. "You haven't explained the missing training schedules. Chief, if I didn't know you, I'd think you were in need of a psych eval for talking like this."

Cassidy wasn't so sure she didn't need just that, especially after that little exchange with Shane. She stood, dread seeping into her gut. "I want to see Anderson the second he walks through the door. He doesn't talk to anybody. He doesn't get to stash his gear. His feet hit the parking lot, he's in my office."

"What exactly do you think is going on?"

She certainly wasn't about to address the fact that it looked more and more like somebody was running drugs through their supply lines. He might actually start to believe she was a head case. "I'm not exactly sure. But one way or another, I've been played."

"We talked to the police about the break-ins last night. Maybe it's time to turn the rest of this over to the authorities." Shane sank into the chair Mac had vacated and reached for the printed inventory.

"I don't know. Those mismatched numbers don't prove anything except that someone out there got sloppy with their paperwork." He opened his mouth to say something, but Cassidy kept talking. "You turned over more than this the first time, and nothing happened. I don't want to look like the boy who cried wolf."

As she watched Shane roll the papers and tap them against his thigh, she was struck by the other reason she didn't want to give up their search yet. Doing so would leave him with no reason to stay in her life.

Her lungs worked harder for oxygen, and she circled her desk to put space between them. No, she would not make judgment calls based on misguided memories and a kiss born of overwrought emotions.

"You okay?"

She didn't look up as she dropped into her desk

chair. "I'm fine." The words were snappier than she'd meant them to be, telegraphing that she was anything but "fine." Cassidy yanked open her top desk drawer to look for her ibuprofen, but a knock on her door stilled her hand.

Master Sergeant McIntyre stood in the doorway with Private Anderson.

Shoving all thoughts into a dark corner, she motioned for the pair to enter her office.

McIntyre stepped out as Shane rose and took a position near the door. Anderson stood before her desk, shoulders back and posture at attention. Tension poured off the kid in waves. His eyes couldn't stay focused in one spot but darted around the room seeking a target to lock on.

After the moment had dragged out long enough, Cassidy stood, rounded her desk and motioned for Shane to shut the door.

The private flinched as the door clicked.

Cassidy straightened her shoulders and looked at Shane. Their silent conversation told her he thought the same thing she did. This soldier was guilty of something bigger than a botched upgrade to his vehicle.

Leaning against the desk a few feet from her soldier, Cassidy crossed her arms and leveled her gaze on him. "So, Private, care to tell me why you're here?"

His eyes flicked to her and forward again. "Ma'am, I have no idea."

"Mmm-hmm. Maybe you can answer a question for me." She pursed her lips and lifted the doctored manifest from her desk. "Who would want to torch your vehicle?"

Cassidy could tell the moment the words filtered through. Anderson's jaw tensed, and his eyes popped slightly wider. His skin went pale so fast she feared he'd slump to the floor.

"So you believe somebody had a reason to do that?"

"I— It's—" His gaze bounced from Cassidy to Shane and back.

The kid was going to bolt. Cassidy straightened. As she did, Shane read the situation and moved to stand directly in front of the door.

Beads of sweat marched across Anderson's forehead. "Chief...I can't."

Cassidy's knees weakened. She gripped the desk behind her, trusting it would hold under the weight of her shock. It couldn't be, but this really was happening. Time stretched tight, like she was in a nightmare where she wanted to scream, wanted to run, but nothing would allow her to move. She inhaled and willed her brain to function. Pulling through time and calling on every ounce of her training, she stiffened her spine and drew up her chin. "You can't what?"

Her hesitation had given Anderson time to regain

his composure. "It was nitrous, Chief. That's what all of the reports say."

Cassidy dug her fingernails into the wood underneath the edge of her desk and tried to force the private off his footing again. She fired a shot without aiming, hoping it would hit the target. "And what did you do to my computer?"

There it was again. A moment of sheer terror raced through Anderson's dark eyes. His Adam's apple bobbed. "I— I fixed it."

"Try again." Putting on her strictest command face, Cassidy stepped closer. She hadn't been a hundred percent sure her computer problems at the office were tied into everything else, but his reaction told her all she needed to know. Still, they needed more before they could pick up the phone and call Criminal Investigation. If he didn't crack and say something incriminating, they had only his reactions, and that bought them nothing. "You sabotaged it first. And if you didn't, you know who did."

"We've had systems issues due to an upgrade in our security software. I replaced your CAC reader and uploaded… I mean, updated your security software. Easy fix." He looked at her, eyes pleading. "That's all. It had nothing to do with the chip in your ID card. Just the reader."

Cassidy felt her eyelid twitch. The chip in her ID card? What was he talking about? The kid was flipping out. "You're sticking with that story?"

"That's what happened, Chief."

A pounding headache began behind Cassidy's left eye and spread into her cheek. It was like trying to dig a hole in a bucket of water, and she wasn't up to the task. "We'll discuss this later, but this isn't over. Go join your formation. You can go."

"Yes, Chief." Anderson was gone before Cassidy could blink.

Shane shut the door behind him. "Surely you aren't buying what he said."

"Not even close. He's up to something and scared to death we're going to figure out what it is."

"He's not the guy I saw break into your house either time. Could he have been the one you grabbed the other night?"

Cassidy's stomach tightened. She hadn't wanted to go that far, although the idea had circled like a vulture. "I don't know." And for the first time in her life, she had no idea which way to turn next.

The brightness of the midday sun angled into the room through the blinds, striping the carpet with light and shadow. Shane sat forward in the desk chair, elbows on his knees, and watched Derek twist screws in the cover of Cassy's computer.

Cassy leaned against the closet door behind him, fidgeting with the beret in her hands.

Shane avoided looking at her as much as possible. Every time he'd been around her today, he'd been focused on other people, other things. When she'd come into the room behind him just now, he was struck anew by the sight of her in her ACUs. The strength Cassy exuded when she was in uniform had never failed to swell his heart. In better times, Shane had been amazed by the difference between strict, by-the-book Cassy in uniform and soft, laughing Cassy in jeans and a T-shirt. Civilian Cassy was the side of her he'd once considered all his own.

He swallowed hard and shifted in the chair. For that brief moment last night she'd been all his again, and the memory pulsed in the room, making the air hard to breathe. She'd nearly been kidnapped last night. A kiss was the last thing he needed to dwell on.

When she'd come in, Shane had offered the seat to her, but she'd refused. After Cassy greeted Derek, she retreated to where she now stood and hadn't said another word. Either she was still feeling the physical and mental bruises from last night, or the whole situation had taken a toll on her peace of mind.

Her breathing was soft behind him, and her presence brushed his senses even though she was several feet away. Shane focused his attention with laser-guided precision on the activity in front of him in an effort to block memories both old and new. "You found anything yet?"

"Man, you have to give me more than three seconds to take a look." Derek grinned and shook his head as he flipped the computer's outer case, then handed it to Shane. "I don't see anything, but you can check behind me if it'll keep you quiet."

"Thanks." Shane snatched the metal cover from Derek and ran his hands over the inside, letting his eyes trail his fingers. Everything looked like he'd imagine the inside of a computer's hard shell should. "Nothing." He held it out to Cassy, but she shook her head, attention locked on Derek's work.

"I know." The words were strained as Derek bent over the inner workings of the computer. "Just figured it'd give you something to do. Make you feel useful."

Cassy snorted a short laugh.

Even though the laugh was at his expense, Shane let a smile twitch the corners of his mouth. Amusement was better than the silent shell she'd retreated into. "Hush up, both of you. Of all people, you two ought to know it's not easy to sit on the sidelines and watch."

"Um, no." Cassy's voice held a familiar teasing edge that catapulted him back to better days. "You're the absolute worst when you're not in the middle of something. You can't stand to be benched and forced to watch other people do the grunt work."

Shane twisted the chair around to look at her, half stung by the gibe, half shocked she'd been comfortable enough to say it.

Derek spoke before Shane could retort. "Ain't that

the truth. He just wants to be the hero, that's all. You know, the guy who swoops in to save the day? Can't do that when you're not doing the work."

"See?" Cassy arched an eyebrow and pointed to Derek. "I'm telling the truth."

Shane's eyes riveted onto hers. Behind the exhaustion and the worry, laughter sparked. It was a look he thought he'd never see aimed at him again. He held his breath, afraid if he moved she'd retreat behind the wall she'd been busy cementing around her.

"The boy has a hard time sitting still and waiting, that's for sure." Derek's voice drew Cassy's gaze.

Shane sucked in a deep breath. For the first time in his life, he wanted to shove a gag in his best friend's mouth. He was certain Derek hadn't meant anything by the words, but the implication he'd strayed hovered in the room. Cassy's face drew tight. Her eyes cloaked. Shane turned to Derek and sought a way to lighten the air. "Better watch out. I'll tell some of your daredevil war stories to your girlfriend."

"I'll have to find one first." Derek spoke around the small screwdriver he held between his teeth. His eyes roamed the machine in front of him, taking in every wire and chip. It was a long time before he broke the tense silence in the room. "Nothing." He pulled the screwdriver from his mouth and scratched his cheek. "There's not a thing here that shouldn't be here."

"Maybe I just thought somebody moved it." Cassy's voice oozed self-doubt. "With all that's happened, it could just be I'm looking for things to be wrong."

Shane pushed himself out of the chair and went to the window. He shoved his hands in his pockets and stared down at the front lawn, where the grass stiffened and crisped in the July drought. He could feel her slipping away. "Except I saw them sneak in the side door, and they were in the house when you got home."

"True."

"Okay," Derek said. "I'll give you that one. But who says it's about the computer? It could be, but it might also be to throw you off the real trail. You know the drill, man. If you want to hide something, throw the evidence toward something else. There could be anything, anywhere in this house."

Even though she stood a few feet from him, Shane could sense Cassy stiffen. He turned from the window in time to watch Derek twist the last screw into the side of the computer.

"I'll run a scan on the hard drive, but I'll bet there's nothing there." Derek stood and shoved the computer into its place under the desk. "Not to jump off the deep end or anything, but you need to consider something." He looked at Cassy. "If you're really in danger, what they might have left in this house could cause a lot more damage than a bug in a computer."

Cassy sucked in a quick breath.

There were too many questions without answers, too many places danger could hide. For the first time since Cassy left him, Shane felt like he couldn't win, like he'd lost control of the situation. Cold fear steeled his muscles. "No."

"It wouldn't take a big explosive, dude. And there's a million places to hide something."

As Shane turned to the window, he caught a quick glimpse of Cassy's face. She no longer leaned against the closet door but stood at full attention, her expression unreadable. He gripped the window frame and let his eyes roam the street below. There could be a dozen different threats in the house. "We need to find somewhere safer for you."

"No." The word was a harsh echo of his own exclamation.

Shane whipped toward her. "Cassy, if there's anything here that's meant to…hurt you, we'd never find it without equipment. You can't play around—"

"I said no." The start-up melody of the computer overlaid her response. "You need to get a grip on reality. What exactly do you want me to do? Go AWOL? Quit my job? You can't be my bodyguard. And you can't force me underground. I have a job to do. So far the only real damage that's been done is to Anderson's car."

"And you've been attacked twice," Derek muttered.

Cassy ignored him and jabbed her finger in the direction of the stairs. "Think about what you're saying, both of you. You can't seriously believe there's a...a *bomb* here. Blowing up my house would never work without raising a boatload of suspicion. This place is completely electric. There's no gas line running to the house to pin an explosion on. I don't even have a gas grill with a propane tank. Whoever this is has already had a chance to take me out. Twice. They didn't take it."

"She's got a point," Derek said.

Shane wanted to kick him. He paced the room and stood behind Derek at the computer, staring at the virus scan's progress meter on the screen. If he didn't get a grip on his emotions soon, he'd jump straight into loony land imagining all of the possible negative scenarios, or he'd find himself tearing this house apart nail by nail. Situations like this were the precise reason emotions couldn't come into play on a mission. They messed with your reasoning.

When it came to Cassy, his emotions ran the show, and at a time like this he needed his head to coach the game. "Fine. You're right. My interpreter said these guys are setting up a major operation. They're not going to risk it by doing something to draw a lot of attention or raise too much suspicion. If they do decide they need to take care of any problems, it'll be quieter than that." He kneaded the back of his neck as possibilities raced through his mind. Facing Cassy, he took a step closer and forced her to meet his eyes. "And that's what scares me."

"It scares you because you're paranoid." Cassidy ignored the ferocity in Shane's expression. She'd seen that look before. It said he'd protect her to the death if he had to. It had been a long time since anyone had looked at her that way.

And she certainly wished she didn't find comfort in Shane doing it now. "Listen, both of you. I think—"

"Uh-oh." Derek's voice ceased every motion in the room. Cassidy's last words hung in the air, thought unfinished while Shane continued to stare at her.

Closing her eyes and shaking her head, Cassidy eased around Shane to Derek. "*Uh-oh* is never good."

"That's an understatement," Shane muttered behind her, before raising his voice. "What's wrong?" He stepped closer, and while he didn't touch Cassidy, she was keenly aware of the bulk of his chest just inches from her back, his breath warm on her neck.

Derek clicked through several screens Cassidy had never seen before, then pointed to a line that was nothing but gibberish to her. "Without giving you a lecture on computer guts..." He inhaled deeply. "It looks like someone tried to change your IP address."

"Speak English, not computer geek." Shane chuckled, though it stretched thin.

Cassidy half smiled, grateful for the moment of levity even as her heart sank low enough to beat inside her boots.

There wasn't a trace of amusement in Derek's voice. "Simply put, somebody tried to re-identify your computer to the internet. Either they're trying to hide something you did, or they're trying to make it look like you did something you didn't." He swiveled the chair to look up at Cassidy. "Either way, it's proof somebody's after you."

TEN

Shane squinted through the windshield against the heat that radiated in waves off the asphalt. It'd be nice if this were a mirage. He jerked his sunglasses away from his face, swiped at them with his T-shirt and shoved them into place. Nope, it didn't change a thing. Not fifty feet away from him, in the parking lot of a gas station just outside post, stood Cassy's Jackson.

But it wasn't Jackson who tightened every muscle in his body in a mix of hot and cold anger. It was the man sitting on the motorcycle talking with him. Shane was sure that face would haunt his vision every time he felt the scar forming on his arm. Even now, the pain dug into his triceps with more pulse than usual. It was pain he deserved for allowing uncertainty to silence his intuition.

He clenched his jaw, half wishing he'd skipped the burger he'd downed at lunch because it lay like cement in his gut. It had been one thing to speculate about Jackson's involvement, but it was another thing to track him down at work and follow him for an afternoon. To see proof in front of his face in broad daylight made him want to climb out of his truck and beat the man into the ground. The heat of his rage terrified him. If he tried to confront Jackson right now, it was likely he'd whale on him until there was nothing left but blood on his fists.

God, help me. It was the best prayer he could send up. No other words would come, and it would sure take the power of God to keep him calm.

What would this do to Cassy? She already believed she couldn't trust anyone. A betrayal of this magnitude was liable to drive her so far into herself that she never came out. It was a cold thought and something he could not let happen.

A flurry of motion between the two men recaptured Shane's attention. They clasped hands, then Jackson climbed into his dark BMW sedan and took off toward post. The other man tilted his head to slip on his helmet, stopped, pulled a cell phone from his pocket and studied the screen.

Shane didn't even breathe. He'd parked in an out-of-the-way spot, but he was still in the line of sight, and if he moved at all it would bring attention to himself. He didn't doubt the motorcycle rider would know who he was in an instant. But the longer he sat, the bigger Jackson's head start. The moments passed until he lost all hope of catching up to the other man.

Finally, the rider strapped his helmet on and roared across the parking lot right past Shane.

He stiffened. If the guy saw him…

There didn't seem to be any hesitation in the rider as he gunned his engine and merged into traffic headed toward Fayetteville.

Shane exhaled loudly. He debated following the motorcycle, but he'd lost the heart to do it. All he could think of was getting the truth to Cassy as soon as he could. He snatched his cell phone and stared at the screen. The burden of it weighed heavy against his palm. If Cassy had any feelings for Jackson, she could sever all ties right now and there'd be no way to protect her. Worse, she could tell Jackson and put herself in immediate danger. But if he didn't tell her…

He shook his head. No, she had to know so she could protect herself. And as much as he wished he could tell her in person, she needed to know now. Pressing his lips together, he yanked her number out of his pocket and dialed.

Still nothing. Cassidy scrolled through the files on her work computer, looking for anything out of place, anything that would indicate it had been tampered with. Everything looked normal. It made no sense. Maybe Anderson was telling the truth and her CAC reader had gone bad. Even if that was the case, it took only one number out of the equation. All of the rest still failed to add up.

Convinced she needed a long vacation, she powered down the computer. It was almost time to meet Jackson for an early dinner. She'd agreed to it the previous evening. Before more people broke into her house. Before her computer gave up its secrets. Before she kissed Shane. With a sigh big enough to blow papers across her desk, she planted her palms on the flat surface and pushed herself up. Her spirit weighed so much it felt like she wore Kevlar body armor. It would be better if she rain-checked Jackson. His sudden flurry of interest was more than she could handle.

Jackson. He'd asked her out Friday and last night—the same two nights her house had been invaded. Cassidy sank back into her chair, knees refusing to hold her any longer. He'd borrowed her laptop, worked with computers and had been the one to find her "missing" ID card on Friday. Dread seeped bile into her stomach.

It had nothing to do with the chip in your ID card. Anderson's words slapped her with new force. What if it had everything to do with the chip in her ID card? Someone tried to access her computer between the explosion Friday afternoon and the start of business Monday, and they'd need her ID and password to do it. It had failed in the morning but had worked again after Anderson borrowed it to check the settings on her new CAC reader yesterday.

She pulled her ID from her pocket and studied it. It looked fine. It was always on her person, it couldn't have been tampered with or switched… The only time it had been out of her sight was Friday when she left it in the machine to rush downstairs and Jackson found it on the floor.

Her fingers numbed, and she fumbled the card in her hand. It was a tenuous connection, but it made far too much sense. She had to find Shane and get his reaction.

She slung her laptop bag onto her shoulder and jogged down the stairs.

Private Walker met her at the bottom. "All clear to lock up, Chief?"

Her feet dragged to a stop and braked her thoughts as well. "What are you doing here, Walker? I thought you were gone over an hour ago."

"Locking up. Sergeant Winchester and I are handling it tonight."

The thump of her heart echoed through her body. "You're on the duty roster for Thursday. I just looked at it a few minutes ago."

"I was, ma'am. But Anderson offered me fifty bucks to switch nights with him. He's got money to burn lately, and I ain't turning down that kind of cash just to lock up two days earlier than I was supposed to. I'd have to be crazy. Sergeant Landon's got lockup that night and, to be honest, I think he's got a little crush on her. Seems like they're always whispering together about something. It's like high school all over again."

Cassidy's mouth went dry. Anderson again. Switching lockup so he'd be one of the last two people in the building on Thursday, the night the shipping containers came in. Throwing around money "to burn." And now he was involved with Landon. Her eyes refused to focus, and she swayed, then regained her footing. Too much, too fast.

"You okay, Chief?" His hand hovered near her elbow, like he wanted to help but was afraid to touch his superior.

"Yeah. Long day. Don't blame you for taking his money." Even though she tried to make her voice nonchalant, it came out high and thin. "Have a good night." She slipped on her sunglasses and pushed through the door, her focus set on her Trailblazer parked near the road at the end of the building. That was it. She'd find Shane, put this all together and call Criminal Investigation. Then she'd hope that when she awoke in the morning, all of it was a drawn-out, vivid nightmare.

Surprise almost made her skip a step. It was a nightmare that breathed. Private Anderson stood by her driver's side door.

She recovered her composure and strode toward him with purpose. All roads led to this kid, and here he was again. Her earlier feeling of suffocation came back with a vengeance, and she had the claustrophobic sensation that everything in her life was drawing to a sharp point.

Anderson slumped, then straightened, fear and uncertainty etching even deeper lines on his face than they had in her office.

"Private." Cassidy unlocked the doors of the vehicle and stowed her laptop in the backseat, trying to project authority, not the rattled, fear-tinged chaos she truly felt. She shut the door and focused on the soldier. "Is there something I can help you with?"

"It's about your computer, Chief."

Adrenaline vibrated in her fingertips. "Go on."

"I...didn't tell you the truth today." Like a swooping bird, his eyes darted to her and away again.

Cassidy stifled a sarcastic retort and crossed her arms. "Is that so? Then what's the real story?" Her voice was even, although her heartbeat skipped and stuttered. His answer could unlock more than she could ever imagine.

"Well, when I was—"

"Cass, there you are." Jackson's voice bellowed across the parking lot.

Cassidy's mouth went dry. Here she stood between questions and danger, with nothing but an empty parking lot between them. Her toes curled in her boots. She turned away from the young private to face Jackson, hoping her face wouldn't betray her anxiety. "Hey. I need five minutes."

"Sure." Jackson pointed across the parking lot toward the building. "I'm parked over there."

Her knees nearly gave way with relief. They weren't tag-teaming her. She waited for Jackson to get a few feet away, then turned to Private Anderson, the corner of her eye still keeping tabs on the man she was beginning to suspect was anything but a friend. "You were saying?"

"Nothing, ma'am." He swallowed so hard that his Adam's apple rebounded like a basketball. "Nothing that can't wait until tomorrow."

Cassidy stifled a groan. Not when she was so close. Options spun like dust in a helicopter's rotor wash. As his superior, she could order him to talk, but forcing the words out of him would probably make him retreat the same way he had in her office. She glanced across the parking lot at Jackson. Paranoia controlled her thinking. Jackson was safe. She'd known him too long and too well. So Anderson had gone mute at the sight of him. Most likely, the kid didn't want to talk in front of someone else. As much as she wanted answers, she had to admit to temporary defeat. There was no way to get what she needed with expediency, and patience wasn't a virtue she had a lot of. "Private, I'll be in tomorrow morning at 0530. I expect you to be waiting at my office door."

Anderson met her gaze. "Understood, Chief."
Without another word or a backward glance, the
soldier bolted around the corner of the rigger shed.

Cassidy squeezed her eyes shut. She needed a
door, a window, some opening to let the light shine
on all of this madness. It didn't seem to matter which
way she turned. All she saw were walls.

The jangle of her cell phone jerked her attention.
Holding one finger up to Jackson where he waited
in his car, she yanked the cell from her leg pocket,
punched the answer key and whipped the phone to
her ear, feeling like the fox within sniffing distance
of the hounds. If this mess continued, she'd have to
quit caffeine or have a heart attack, one or the other.
"Chief Matthews."

"Cassy, it's Shane."

All noise around her ceased. Every particle in
her body focused on the sound of his voice on the
line. It had been so many years since she'd heard his
voice isolated over the telephone. She'd forgotten
how it sounded. Deep, confident, just enough drawl
to reach through the earpiece and play on memories
she thought she'd forgotten. Life stopped swirling,
and she grabbed a shred of peace.

"Cassy? You okay?"

"We need to talk." She shook her head. "But right
now—" The words broke off as Jackson stepped up
and Shane interrupted her.

"Listen to me. I know you aren't going to want to,

but you have to." His exhale blew through the line with such force she expected it to twitch the hair away from her ear. "Jackson's in on it."

On her first tour in Iraq, an IED detonated under the convoy vehicle in front of hers. The concussion had stolen her breath, the blast so loud it had not only deafened her but blinded her for that split instant of sound. Shane's words hit her with the same force. The world went dark and silent. Her phone slipped through her fingers and crashed to the pavement. Everything rushed back with a roar that echoed in her ears.

"Cass?" Jackson gripped her shoulders. "Look at me." He pointed to his eyes, then clasped her shoulder again. "Right here. Are you okay?"

Breath stuttering, Cassidy lifted her gaze and focused on the eyes in front of her. For the first time since she'd met her closest friend, they were the eyes of a total stranger.

Cassidy sat on the edge of the couch, back stiff, eyes surveying Jackson's apartment.

"You're like a prowling lion." Jackson sat on the coffee table in front of her, his gaze probing hers. "You sure you don't want to talk about it?"

"You should have let me drive home. I'd have been fine." Fear zipped up and down her spine, and her survival instinct dialed up to eleven. Why hadn't she fought him when he urged her into his car? Cassidy rolled her eyes skyward. Because she'd been shocked beyond reasonable thought. "I told you. It was…bad news."

"Your house didn't get broken into again, did it?"

"No." His proximity made her feel like she was shackled into place. Sliding sideways on the sofa, she hefted herself to her feet and walked to the window. "Why didn't you just let me go home?"

"I wasn't going to let you drive home in that condition."

"Can we forget dinner? Take a…a rain check?" If her earlier suspicions were right and Shane had real basis for his accusation, her caged prisoner act would tip the balance of suspicion into Jackson's favor. She had to get a hold of herself and play this like she knew nothing. And she couldn't do that on her own. She couldn't remember the last time she'd prayed, but the thought spun out in a way so natural she couldn't stop it. *A little help here, God? Just enough calm to get me out of here without getting into worse trouble?*

Peace settled over her. For the first time in her life, the strength came from somewhere outside of her. In a way she couldn't express, her heart slowed, her breathing paced itself, her voice steadied. She turned from the window to find Jackson standing by the couch wearing a look that crossed between annoyance and frustration. "I'm sorry. You think I'm a total flake, don't you?"

A flash of something she couldn't read crossed Jackson's face, then he pulled his hands from his pockets and produced her phone. Hours passed as he studied the device, then glanced at her and down again. Finally, he ran his thumb over the screen, then held the phone out to her. "Here. You dropped it on my toe."

"Sorry. Thanks." Her fingertips grasped the phone, still warm from his grip. If Jackson was the bad guy in all this, the one who was out to "smoke" whoever was in her position if things went south, why give her phone back? Right now was the perfect time to take her out if that was his intention. No one knew where she was. There were no witnesses. It didn't make sense.

"Look, I'll go change into some shorts, then I'll take you to your car. We'll grab dinner another night. Or lunch the day after tomorrow. That work for you?"

"Sure." The edge wore off her adrenaline. She had her phone, and he was leaving her alone. No way was he planning to harm her, at least not right now.

Jackson rounded the couch and stopped at the end of the hallway. The look in his eyes wasn't one she'd ever seen before. With a slow exhale, he turned and disappeared around the corner.

As soon as she heard the bedroom door click shut behind Jackson, Cassidy stuffed her phone in her pocket. What she was about to do was stupid. It was so far past stupid, it headed straight down the highway through the gilded gates of insanity.

Clenching her fingers, she let her eyes rest on the desk in the small office off the den. She glanced up the hall and chewed her lower lip. There was no way she was contemplating this, was there?

Too much moved too fast in her life. With a deep breath, she resigned herself to digging through Jackson's life and playing detective. Now might be her only chance, and there was no room for regret if this slipped by. If Shane was right, the outcome was death for one or both of them. If Shane was wrong, she could lose the only real friend she'd had in years. At the moment, neither option seemed palatable.

With one last look toward the hallway, Cassidy stepped into the alcove. It appeared to be a normal home office, except it was ordered with military precision. The only thing that stood out of place was a blue sticky note anchored to the side of the computer screen with a Freemail address and what was probably the password underneath. Snatching a sheet of paper from a pad, she jotted it down, then flipped through the papers on the desk. Light bill, cable bill, cell phone bill… She scanned the list of numbers, and her own jumped out as the most called. Only one other repeated enough to be important. Probably his mother.

His mother. He'd mentioned her in passing a few times, but Cassidy had never met her. The phone bill slipped from Cassidy's fingers as she stared at the top of the desk, then leaned out the doorway to glance at the rest of the apartment. No souvenirs or cards or personal correspondence. No photos of family or friends anywhere. The place could be a hotel room for all the personality it had. In the past she'd chalked it up to his being a guy, but now it seemed more sinister. It looked too much like a showplace, perfectly decorated, flawlessly coordinated, but no personality.

Just how much did she know about Jackson? He was divorced, like her. His father was dead. Like hers. He was from a small town. Like her. He'd played basketball in high school...

Like her. Facts about him fell like dominoes in neat little rows around her. Too neat. Too much about his life mirrored her own.

Her fingers shook as she set the phone bill on the desk. They had so much in common, and every single piece of information about him was tied in a neat little bow. It was all unbelievably perfect.

Suspicion quickly doused guilt. Her earlier thoughts were right. *Shane* was right. Without second-guessing her motives, Cassidy flicked the mouse just enough to wipe away the computer's screen saver.

Her stomach leaned sideways. Her name lay scattered across the screen, in a list of files. She clicked one open and her heart shrunk as she read a record of how she'd spent the past few days, where she'd been, who she'd talked to… All in a memo addressed to…

The breath caught in her throat. Department of Homeland Security? What?

"And just what do you think you're looking at?" The voice over her shoulder hit her ears like a steel baseball bat.

Drawing her upper lip between her teeth, Cassidy closed her eyes and waited a beat before she faced Jackson and jabbed her finger toward the computer screen, opting to play offense. "How about you tell me?" Her voice stayed steady, but if he looked hard enough, he'd read her apprehension.

A blip of uncertainty crossed his face, and something that looked like fear flickered in his expression. His eyes never leaving hers, he reached around her and flicked off the computer monitor. He towered over her, his face inches from hers.

"What's going on, Jackson?"

Jackson cursed under his breath and took a step back, running his hand through his hair. His brown eyes darkened and narrowed. With a harsh breath, he turned and paced to the middle of the room, back rigid.

Cassidy edged out of the office and eyed the door, once again keenly aware she no longer carried a gun at her hip. She wasn't even sure if she needed one. If he was with DHS undercover—investigating her—then his cover was blown. There was no telling what his orders were in this sort of situation. Her mind spun in a thousand different directions, and she grasped the first coherent words that blew past. "Who are you reporting on me to?" Nausea broke over her in a wave of cold sweat. "You're not— Who are you?"

Nothing. His back stayed toward her, a wall of silence.

"Suffice it to say, you're not Jackson Reese. And you're not the friend to me that you pretended to be." Regret gripped Cassidy's heart in a fist. She'd just lost the one person she'd trusted. How could this be happening to her again? "It was all a lie." The whisper fell from her tongue and drifted to her own ears in a brittle hush.

Exhaling loudly, Jackson turned toward her and fixed his eyes on a spot above her head.

"All of it? Everything? Your father and your divorce and where you went to school and…and all of those times you let me spill my guts to you? Every bit of it was calculated to get into my head?" It was too much to take in. She wanted to slide to the floor and bury her face in her knees, but she wouldn't let him see her collapse. "Why?" She swallowed the lump crowding her throat.

Jackson flared his nostrils and pressed his lips together.

"You're already outed. You might as well tell me."

"I can't—" He dropped to the edge of the couch and rested his elbows on his knees, staring at the floor. The silence stretched like a tightrope. "Somebody's running drugs through the supply lines."

"Into my company. I know."

Jackson jerked his head up. "You do?"

"Yes."

"Who told you?" He leaped up and stepped closer, looming over her.

Cassidy refused to shrink even as she debated telling him everything from the time Shane appeared among her winter coats, but she bit back the words. There was no reason to show all of her cards. He probably knew more than she did. "I just found out this week."

"How? Are you working with anybody?"

"Listen, you follow me. You've been around me. You know every single person I talk to and hang out with. The only person I see enough to work with on anything is…you." The word was like a headlock, blocking her next breath.

"You're not making this easy for me."

"Why should I?" He certainly hadn't gone easy on her.

With a loud exhale, Jackson stood and brushed past her into the office. He snatched a folder from the desktop and shoved it into her hand. "These are emails we're still decrypting. It's possible they're nothing, but also possible they're details on supply routes, buyers and sellers. Chief Matthews, they came from your personal email accounts."

ELEVEN

"You've reached Cassidy Matthews, leave a message after—"

Shane stabbed the end button on the cell phone and hurled it to the couch in the trailer. It bounced off the cushion and landed on the floor. He wanted to kick it, but the most that would get him was a trip to the store for a new one.

Cassy had hung up on him when he told her about Jackson, just like he feared she would. There was no telling where she was now. She wasn't answering her cell phone. There was no clue where to look for her. He stalked to the window and peered through the blinds. With all that was going on, he could only hope she was simply off somewhere stewing, out of the way of immediate danger. But he had no way to know.

Shoving his hands into the pockets of his khaki cargo shorts, he clenched his fists. If he were in a firefight, he'd know exactly what to do. There were tactical maneuvers, positions he could take, moves he could plot. When it came to the situation with Cassy, his brain short-circuited. He didn't know whether to dodge right or deflect left, to look up or duck down. If he stayed at the house, he could miss a chance to help her. If he left, he could miss her altogether.

He pressed his fist against the window casing and started to push away, but a flash caught his eye in the evening sun. Cassy's Trailblazer crept up the street. It wasn't until the air left his body in a rush that he realized he'd been holding his breath. As the garage door rose, his muscles relaxed. She was okay.

This time.

When Cassy stepped out of the car, she stopped short at the sight of him. "Where have you been all afternoon?"

"Following Jackson."

"Well, you didn't follow him far enough." Her voice flattened as she turned away from him and stalked across the garage into the house.

Shane followed her through the kitchen and into the den. Something was definitely wrong. He could see it in the set of her jaw and the line of her shoulders.

Cassy set her laptop case against the end of the couch and dropped her mail onto the coffee table. "I can take care of myself."

Shane wanted to throw his arms around her and hold her tight, but he knew better than to make a move toward her. Instead, he shoved his hands into his pockets and watched as she settled onto the couch and untied her boots. "Where have you been?"

"Oh, I'm sorry. I forgot to call home, *Dad,* and tell you I'd be late. Do you want to ground me? Confiscate my cell phone? Force me to go into hiding from drug runners?" Her voice hardened.

Reflexes jerked his head like he was dodging a blow. He'd expected anger, some sort of backlash, but not this kind of venom. Something had happened. "You okay? If this has to do with what I told you about—"

"I'm fine. And I don't need you to protect me." She bent to work on her other boot, and her voice muffled. "You can drop back. I'll be fine."

"No."

Cassy's fingers stilled on her bootlaces. She looked frozen in time. "What did you say?" She addressed the floor, never lifting her eyes to meet his.

"No."

She inhaled deeply, then stood, drawing herself up to what Shane knew was her tallest, most commanding pose. "You can leave. Everything's taken care of."

He shook his head and kept his voice even. For all the world, this felt like talking down a rabid dog. "What does that mean? You went to CID? Back to the police? What?"

"It means…" She swallowed hard and refused to meet his eyes. "It means it's taken care of."

Shane rocked back on his heels. "Until I know you're really safe, I'm not going anywhere."

"Safe from whom?"

"Jackson? And his motorcycle riding cohort?"

"Leave Jackson out of this. He's not the problem. He apparently never was."

He wanted to pull off the gloves and throw this thing down once and for all, but now was the worst time. Her life had a fast-approaching expiration date if he didn't focus. And he was the only one who could save her.

"Cassy." Shane's words stunk of manufactured calm. "You're angry, and I have a pretty good idea it's not at me."

His presumption cranked the gas under her rage. "Not about you? My life was great until you sprung into it. I was so far past you, you weren't even in my rearview mirror anymore. I didn't have traitors running around in my company and inventories that didn't match and privates lying to me, and Jackson was a friend and not a—a—" She sucked in a deep breath and tried to beat back the pounding in her temples.

"I'm sorry Jackson's in on it."

Cassy's head popped up, and she searched for any sign of sarcasm. There was none. Nothing but compassion reflected in his green eyes. And his sympathy undid her.

Tears crept onto her lashes and stung her nose. Cassidy blinked in surprise at the emotion. It swept on her as suddenly as a summer thunderstorm, and she couldn't stop the words that poured from her mouth. "I was with Jackson when you called. You were right and wrong about him. He's involved, but not like you think, and I can't tell you what's going on. But I was driving home and I realized... I can't talk to him anymore." She sniffed and swallowed her tears, hating herself for the words but not able to stop them. "You're the only person I ever really trusted, and you betrayed me. But now you didn't really betray me, and I was the stupid one. And now there's nobody. All I've got is you, and I don't even know if I want you." She sank to the step behind her and challenged Shane with her eyes.

He shifted and exhaled loudly, watched her warily, waiting for who knew what.

Dropping her gaze, she ripped open the Velcro pocket of her uniform pants and smashed it shut again. "You disgusted me back then, Shane. Now I..." She ran out of steam and stared at the floor between her knees, wishing the stairs would collapse and bury her.

Shane shifted, and she felt more than heard him move toward her. If he touched her, so help her she'd... Well, honestly, she didn't know what she'd do.

Instead of pulling her to him, he eased onto the step at her feet. She could see him in the edge of her vision, picking fuzz off the carpet. "I'm human." His voice sank lower than her mood. "You're looking for perfection from a person, somebody who's never going to hurt you? Cassy, it's not going to happen."

"I want to be left alone."

"No, you don't. Not really." He turned his attention to the carpet on the step below her. "What happened with Jackson?"

She shrugged. He'd sketched out enough about the investigation to get him relieved of his job if anyone found out, then sworn her to secrecy. "I can't tell you, but he's not a bad guy."

Shane looked like he was going to argue, then his eyes widened. "You're kidding. He's with Criminal Investigation?"

The wall around all of her secrets collapsed. "I don't know which agency, but that's about the size of it." The tears threatened again. "I've trusted one person outside of work in almost ten years. And then I find out…" She couldn't do it. If she let slip the investigation focused on her, Shane might never believe she was the innocent one.

"Is he what's really bothering you?"

"Sort of." The honest answer slipped out before Cassidy could think about it. "No, he's not." She planted her hands on her knees and pushed herself to stand. "I told you. There's nobody to go to with all of this. But you know what?" Taking a deep breath, she stacked more bricks around her heart. "It doesn't matter. I'm a big girl. I can take care of me. I always have."

"Yes, you have." He looked at her and stood. Even though he was still a step below her, she almost had to look up to meet his eye. "But sometimes you have to let somebody else carry the load."

"Like you?" she scoffed. It irked her the way he could read her. He'd always had a sixth sense where she was concerned, and time hadn't dulled it.

"You don't get it, do you?" Shane shook his head and glanced at his watch, then turned and walked down the stairs. "I've got to meet somebody. You want to change clothes and come with me?"

Cassidy opened her mouth and closed it. Guess that conversation was over. "Why?"

He stopped with his hand on the rail and turned to look at her. "Because you might just learn something."

TWELVE

The blinds clicked against the office window as Cassidy dropped them into place. She crossed her arms over her chest and leaned against the wall, glancing at the glowing numbers on the clock across the room: 11:18. She lifted a slat on the blinds and peeked out again, hoping the vision had changed.

Nope. The trailer—with Shane in it—was still out there. She'd give him credit for his tenacity, but that was about the only positive thought she could muster for him after what he'd pulled tonight.

She'd agreed to go with him tonight out of curiosity, and he'd dragged her to a church service.

Church. Since when did Shane Logan darken the threshold of a church? Since when did she? Surely he knew better than to drag her to a prayer meeting, knew how she felt about the way God chose to answer prayer.

So he'd become a Christian. Right. Cassidy had seen more than enough battlefield conversions that didn't last past the first week back in the States.

But those little differences she'd noticed niggled at her brain. The way his temper didn't flare every thirty seconds. The amount of patience he'd shown with her. The difference in his word choices when he got angry. Cassidy wrinkled her forehead. She hadn't heard one foul word out of him, and she'd sure given him enough opportunities to spout off. But still...Shane at church? It was like a leap into a parallel universe.

She made one last peek between the blinds, then tromped down the stairs in her bare feet, still wearing the jeans and T-shirt she'd pulled on before going on Shane's little adventure. When she hit the living room, the weight of the past few days slammed her right in the temple and she sank to the edge of the couch.

The mail still lay on the coffee table where she'd tossed it during her earlier confrontation with Shane. On top of the random jumble of bills and advertisements lay a deep blue flyer with screaming red letters, "We all deserve a second chance." She stared at the ad for auto financing and let the words blur to wavy focus. Second chances. Had she even given Shane a first chance, time to explain the truth?

Fiery realization burned her. Before she could think too hard about what she was doing or could consider the consequences of her actions, Cassidy snatched the ad from the table, threw open the front door and stomped to the trailer where Shane slept.

She pounded on the door, grateful the houses on either side of her were vacant.

It was a minute before he appeared wearing jeans and a PT shirt that fit just tight enough to do battle with her growing attraction. His hair was rumpled, eyes half-awake, but Shane stood ready to defend her as needed. "What's wrong? What happened?"

Cassidy descended the step and stood in the middle of the driveway, her heart pounding in her ears. What she was about to do was either unbelievably humble or supremely stupid. She held up the advertisement as though it would explain everything. "We need to talk."

"We don't have to do this." Shane eyed Cassy across the kitchen table as she plunked down glasses. Even though it had been a long time since he'd had the chance to study her in all of her moods, he still recognized pain behind her eyes. "Seriously, you can stop now."

It was like she didn't hear him. "No, I need to do this."

He complied and watched her hands grip the pitcher as she poured lemonade for both of them. He still wasn't one-hundred-percent sure this was reality. Her summons had roused him from a fitful sleep. When he'd figured out she was muttering about second chances, it had been the cold dash of wakefulness he'd needed. She wanted to hear him out? Now? In the middle of the night while her life was in danger? Either he was still asleep or she'd acquired a twin sister somewhere along the line.

Cassy settled the pitcher onto the table and slid into the chair across from him. "Know what? I've been wrong all week. I've accused you of lying to me, of breaking into my house... And you've been truthful the whole time." Cassy drew her lower lip between her teeth. "Your chaplain friend brought up a good point tonight. If Jesus can know I did wrong and still allow me to come to him and explain and ask for forgiveness, why can't I do that for you? I've been wrong about so much. What if I'm wrong about...everything?"

Jesus? Did she just say *Jesus?* His mind crawled like a turtle while her words flew by on rocket fuel. "Nobody's wrong about everything." Shane studied Cassy as she sipped her drink and studied him right back. It appeared the old Cassy had entered the room, taken charge of the situation and faced it with the will to succeed. She was as bossy as she'd ever been... And as beautiful as she'd ever been.

Long-buried emotions surfaced and gasped for air, pressing against the inside of his rib cage, making it hard for him to take his next breath. He had to beat back the emotions struggling to escape the chains in his chest. No matter what she determined in the next few minutes, their time had ticked away. They may work together to unravel the lies around her, but they'd never be what they once were. Aching realization settled square in his stomach, where it tied barbed wire knots and refused to budge.

Shane swallowed his conflicting emotions and slid into the chair at the end of the table, putting himself at a right angle to Cassy. He took a deep breath, prepared himself for contact and laid his hand on hers. "We really don't have to discuss this now."

She didn't move. For a second, he wondered if she even bothered to breathe. Finally, her eyes met his. "If you ever ran around on me, tell me now, once and for all. Don't drag me through this conversation if you're lying."

Shane drew in a long breath. As much as he wanted to save her the pain he feared she was about to inflict upon both of them by dragging up the past, he wouldn't admit to something he'd never done. "I didn't." He slid the chair back to put space between them and fought to take control of the situation, to feel like he wasn't falling into a drainage canal. "Okay. With everything else going on, this feels like the wrong time, but... Tell me. Tell me why you think I..." He swallowed the words that threatened to choke him. "Why you think there was another woman." Fear seared the back of his neck, mingling with a pain he couldn't identify. It felt like his whole life swung over a fiery pit on a rotten vine, and Cassy could either rescue him or send him plunging to his death. When had she become so important again?

Cassy wrapped both hands around the glass in front of her, gripping so tightly her knuckles faded white. Shane wanted to reach across and pry her fingers away before she shattered the thing in her hands, but her words stilled him. "You were home on leave in South Carolina, and I had to work so I'd stayed at our house. And…I heard you, talking to… whoever she was."

Shane jerked his head back, smugglers and threats on Cassy's life forgotten. When she'd waved papers in his face almost a decade ago, her eyes were determined but dead. Now the flash of pain in them could melt him into vapor if he didn't shield himself. "I don't understand."

"You called me that night, on your cell phone. And I don't know how it happened, but it dialed me after we hung up. And I heard you talking to another woman. I. Heard. Everything." Tears threatened to rush over her eyelashes. "You called me in her presence."

"No." The word rushed out on an exhale as he gripped the edge of the table for support, stomach staging a revolt. "I didn't cheat. Never touched her. We talked about it. But it was all bravado. I couldn't do it. I was a red-level idiot to you, but I wasn't stupid." He leaned forward, elbows on the table, desperate to be in the same space as her. "That was the moment I knew I wanted to fix us, when I realized how far we'd drifted apart. Cassy, I loved you too much." *I still do.* The words throbbed on his tongue, but he bit them in half. The air in the room was too volatile to pitch out a spark like that.

"You didn't?" She sank to the back of her chair, staring at him with eyes that seemed brighter than usual behind unshed tears.

"Never. And I've spent over a decade mad at you for leaving me."

Her shoulders stiffened. "I didn't do anything wrong."

"You gave up on us." His voice dropped lower, the hurt reaching across the years to grab his heart in a fresh grip. "You believed I was the kind of man who'd do something like that."

"I heard—"

"You didn't ask. That's a lack of trust it took me years to get over."

Her gaze grabbed his and wouldn't let him look away. "I should have given you the benefit of an explanation when everything first happened. I should have trusted you. I didn't. So part of this lies with me. I'm sorry."

"You're what?" Her apology came like a left hook.

"I'm sorry. It's just you changed so much after you went Special Forces. I didn't want to hassle with it, didn't want to do the work to keep us together. I'd already made up my mind to leave, and it was just too easy to believe the worst." The refrigerator hummed into the silence between them for several seconds. "It's always bothered me."

"What's that?" The words popped in the air. She was changing the game, and Shane had no idea what his next move should be, or even if he should make one. He cleared his throat, sent a silent prayer for help and tried again. "What's bothered you?"

Her gaze followed her index finger as she ran it down the side of her glass. It was like she couldn't bear to look at him. "I never gave up on anything until that day, when I gave up on the most important thing in my life."

Their eyes locked. The years ebbed away, then Cassy blinked and slipped into business mode. She leveled a softer expression on him before clearing her throat and sliding a folder across the table with two fingers. "Those are the two versions of our container inventories I showed you and Mac this morning. Couple those with the computers and somebody breaking into my house and my office, and you've got every bit of hard evidence we have. Where do we go next?"

Shane's head hurt from the speed with which the conversation switched gears. Clearly, she was done with personal talk, although his heart was just beginning.

Oblivious to his struggle, Cassy kept talking. "I'll tell you… In my own twisted head, I figure if you were telling the truth about something as outrageous as smugglers, you're telling the truth about…her."

"That must be woman logic. No man would ever think that way." He grinned and dropped the inventories on the table, then sat back in his chair in an increasingly vain effort to put distance between them. Having an amicable conversation with her right now was doing more to awaken his emotions than her kiss had the night before. He wasn't sure which was more dangerous—a run-in with potential drug runners or a seat too close to Cassy. He cleared his throat. "Well, tack onto that the fact you found out your friend…isn't your friend, and you've had a rough day."

She flicked the edge of the folder and pressed her lips so tight they turned white around the edges.

"What else is going on?" He could see it. It radiated off her like heat from summer asphalt. She was keeping something from him.

"It's—" Cassy shifted in her seat. "Well, let's just say I know who they believe is behind the smuggling ring."

"Who?"

"Me."

The word shattered like glass. It took a full ten seconds for the full import to set in. "But why would they think—"

"I don't know. Jackson refused to say more. All he showed me were copies of directives asking him to get specific information about me, reports on who I talked to, where I went, court orders to tap my phones…" As she spoke, weight settled and dragged her shoulders toward the floor.

"We'll fight this." In all of his life, Shane had never meant any words more.

"We?" She shook her head. "You'd be better off far away from me. They'll be looking at you next."

"I'm staying."

Cassy blinked rapidly, then raised her eyes to meet his. "Thank you." Her voice was low, but the emotion behind it almost knocked Shane to the floor. "I shouldn't have yelled at you this afternoon. I couldn't control anything, and you know how I hate not having control. Right now, I want to deal with something I can understand." She tapped the papers on the table. "I can understand mismatched inventories, if we put our heads together. One thing at a time. The rest is too overwhelming."

No. Shane wanted to drop everything, grab her by the hand and drag her to the nearest lawyer to defend her. If he were honest with himself, that wasn't the very first thing, but he seriously doubted she'd let him pull her into his arms right now.

She stopped toying with the papers and narrowed her eyes, then flashed him a look of amusement. "I just caught what you said about woman's logic. I'm going to ignore that." The smile slipped from her face. "Do you think it's too late for…" She shook her head and moved to pull her hand away from his side of the table.

Shane instinctively grabbed her fingers, and his heart expanded so fast that it squeezed the air from his lungs. Cassy was tap dancing around a subject he'd hardly dared to hope they'd ever discuss, a place he'd never dreamed they'd go again. And her lips were right there. He ached to close the gap between them. His entire being tightly coiled around his heart, waiting to snap into motion, pull her to him, press his lips to hers...

"Shane."

He felt her whisper more than he heard it as it floated into the space between them.

Her eyes scanned his, speaking things he wasn't entirely sure he understood. *She doesn't understand what she's saying either.* The silent words snapped the spring inside of him, and he flinched. No, he couldn't go back, not when her life was in so much chaos she didn't know which way was up. It wouldn't be fair.

With a deep, shuddering breath, Shane leaned closer, pressed a kiss to her forehead and pulled her to him, trying to hide himself from the confusion in her eyes, knowing what he had to say would cut her. "I can't fix this for you."

Cassy wrapped her arms around his waist and rested her cheek against his chest. "I know."

Shane shook his head, then gently set her away

from him and walked away from her toward the back door, opening a chasm between them. "No, you don't. I can't be your hero. I want to, but I can't. You can't lean on me. I'm the wrong guy."

Confusion crept into her expression. "What?"

"I'll help you any way I can. You know I'm here for you and I'll do everything—" he took a deep breath and gripped the back of his neck before looking into her eyes "—everything in my power to protect you. But I can't be your savior. Do you know when you look at me the way you just looked at me? When you're scared. You think I'm your safe place. And I want to be your safe place, more than I want to breathe. But that's God's job, not mine. And I've overstepped His bounds." He shook his head. "Arrogance. In all of my arrogance I've been trying to fix it all, everything, by myself."

"What are you saying?"

"I don't know." Shane ran his hand down his face and dropped into the chair at the head of the table.

The warmth in Cassy's eyes cooled to stunned confusion. Her lips parted as though she were going to speak, but the chimes of her cell phone ripped through the moment.

She blinked and pulled the phone from the pocket of her jeans in slow motion. She started to say something, then broke eye contact, shook her head and took the call. "This is Matthews."

Shane drew in a deep breath, shoved his emotions

aside and pulled the folder toward him. How anyone had missed the discrepancy was a mystery, but the army was a vast maze of paperwork that jumbled into craziness at times.

"What?" The harsh word burst from Cassy as she shot up, knocking her chair backward. "No."

Shane looked up in time to see the color drain from her face.

"When?" She glanced at him, then walked to the French doors that led to the patio. "Who found him?"

Alarms raced across Shane's nerves. Eyes never leaving Cassy, he eased the folder shut and stood.

"I'm on my way." Her finger trembled as she pressed End, then stared out the window.

"Cassy?"

Swallowing hard, she turned to face him. "Anderson. The kid with the car? Who appears to be at the center of every screwed-up thing that's happening?"

Shane nodded.

"He hung himself."

THIRTEEN

People. All she could see was people.

Cassidy stared out the windshield of Shane's truck as he pulled into her designated parking spot at the rigger shed. He'd insisted she was too shocked to drive. For once she agreed without arguing about it first.

There probably weren't as many people around her buildings as she felt like there were, but in her state of mind, it seemed like half of Fort Bragg swarmed the area.

"Who called all of these people?"

Shane shrugged and tapped the steering wheel with his thumb. "Who knows? It doesn't take much blood in the water to draw folks out, especially when a soldier dies in the relative safety of the States."

Cassidy snorted. "Yeah, okay." She yanked the door handle and stepped out of the truck. "You don't have to hang around. I can get a ride home with Mac."

"I'll stay." Shane turned the keys in the ignition. "If this goes on for a while, you might need me."

"Suit yourself." She shrugged and slammed the door. He could stay as long as he stayed out of the way. He was messing with her emotions to the point she'd nearly asked him for another chance. The way he'd backed away stung. Apparently he didn't feel the same way.

As she strode toward the door, she caught sight of a knot of her soldiers where they stood silent near the road. Cigarette smoke hung in the air around them like the visual representation of the haze in her own head. Apparently, most of them were dragged out of bed by the news, because they looked like a church rummage sale had exploded all over them. If the situation weren't so heartbreaking, she'd laugh at the variety of clothing they'd yanked off the floor in their rush to get here.

Cassidy dipped her head in acknowledgment, but from that distance it was doubtful they could see the small gesture. What else could she do? This was bound to be a defining moment for many of them. They expected things like this in combat. The last thing any young soldier ever assumed was something at home would take them out. They thought they were invincible.

Her mothering instinct gripped her gut. There was nothing she could do to shield them from the hurt.

Specialist Kyle, Private Furst and Sergeant Landon broke away from the group and threaded their way through the cars in the parking lot. Cassidy pressed her lips together and watched them approach, unsure how to answer any questions they might have. She felt like a parent whose children had a raw glimpse of the evening news.

Specialist Anthony Kyle had apparently been appointed group spokesman. "Chief, what's going on?"

"I just got here, Specialist." She let her eyes scan the group and hoped they didn't question her nonanswer.

"Everybody's here except Private Anderson and Sergeant Fisk. Are they okay?" The young sergeant, Erin Landon, the one Anderson purportedly had a crush on, laid a hand on Kyle's shoulder.

Master Sergeant McIntyre appeared in the doorway of the rigger shed, a dark shadow in the harsh light that poured out of the building.

"Sergeant Landon, let the rest of the soldiers know we'll have word for them soon. Until then, you all need to go home and get some sleep." Cassy turned her back on the trio, wishing she could say more, and her steps sped up. "Mac." He moved aside to let her into the small entry at the foot of the stairs. "Fill me in."

"The first sergeant's on the way in. Commander's off on leave." He swallowed hard, face as pale and drawn as she felt, but fell in to match pace with her as she strode down the hallway. Their bootfalls echoed dully as they approached the warehouselike pack room, a premature funeral dirge in the empty building. "Anderson's in the tower."

Her steps faltered. "The shakeout tower? Where we hang the chutes to dry out? But I thought—"

"Yeah, he did. It's not pretty. You sure you want to see this?"

No, she didn't want to see this. She wanted to go home, crawl into bed and pull the covers over her head so far that reality couldn't peek in around the edges. But she had to keep putting one boot in front of the other. As Anderson's superior, she owed it to him not to shy away, to do every last thing in her power to keep his life and death from becoming meaningless. She swallowed hard. "I've seen 'not pretty' more than enough times. This can't be the worst I'll ever see."

Mac stopped walking at the doors that opened onto the pack floor. His gaze fixed on a spot only he could see. "It's the worst I've ever seen."

More than the content of his words, the tone of his voice chilled her blood. The little girl in her wanted to run and not stop until her legs gave out under her, but the grown woman told her to buck up and deal with reality. One of her soldiers had taken his own life. She had to do what she could in the aftermath. If she couldn't be strong, none of her soldiers would handle this well. And none of them would respect her.

"The MPs may confiscate your phone."

The words drew her into the moment. Her pace stuttered. "My phone?"

"Anderson texted me around eight."

Cassidy shook her head. "He texted you? What about his section leader? Why would he break chain of command to—"

"It said, *Don't trust her.*"

"Don't trust who?" Even as the words met air, she knew. One final finger-pointing suspicion in her direction. But why bother to implicate her if he were going to kill himself?

Mac pushed the door open and held it for her to pass into the large room that housed the long wood parachute packing tables. "I don't know. Looks to me like it was cut off in mid-thought."

Even though the closed building held warmth, Cassidy felt frozen to the core as she surveyed the area. Yellow crime scene tape ran across the far end of the room, where doors led to the shakeout tower. MPs stood guard.

She sucked in the humid air and looked at McIntyre. "What do our people know?"

"Officially? Nothing. Unofficially? There's no telling." His eyes never left the tower. "My guess would be all they know is something really, really bad is going on."

Pressing her lips together, Cassidy let her gaze wander to the door to the loading dock, and her attention narrowed into a pinpoint on an ambulance as it pulled up outside. Her stomach tightened and threatened to rush up her throat at the thought of the burden it would soon bear.

One of her soldiers. Dead.

The nerves that pulsed messages from her brain to her legs misfired and left her stuck to the cement floor. Her brain screamed for her to keep moving, but her heart longed for the safety of Shane's arms. Cassidy stiffened her spine. She didn't need a man to support her. And Shane could not be her safe place.

"You ready?" McIntyre still hadn't taken his focus off the doors and the yellow tape in front of them.

"As I'll ever be."

The pair ducked under the crime scene tape and crossed the last few feet as a tall, impossibly thin man stepped between them and the MP shielding the door. He nodded at McIntyre, then leveled his gaze on Cassidy. His eyes scanned every inch of her face, scrutinizing until she felt tempted to look down and make sure her uniform shirt wasn't full of holes. His forehead wrinkled in concentration, making him look like a shar-pei puppy.

The emotion of the day and the absurdity of the thought bubbled a giggle in the back of her throat. She might just turn into a cliché hysterical female if she didn't wake from this nightmare soon.

Seconds passed like days before the man relaxed his forehead and let his gaze wander over her shoulder. It bounced back quickly. "You're Chief Warrant Officer Matthews?"

His demeanor made Cassidy want to point at her rank and name tape and say *Duh*. Instead she nodded, not yet able to trust her voice. Her eyes ached to search past this guy, to see if she could glimpse Anderson and get it over with. At the same time, her legs twitched to run in the opposite direction.

"I'm Special Agent Watters." He flashed a badge, but her brain failed to comprehend anything about it other than it was a shiny object. *Oh, God, restore my sanity...and my voice. I can't hold it together on my own.* For the first time in her life, there was no plan B. She had to trust something bigger than herself or she'd fall on her face and scream.

She cleared her throat, refusing to be the weak woman Agent Watters seemed to expect her to be. "What can you tell us, Special Agent?"

"Not much." He was reading her again, gauging her reactions. Cassidy had no idea if she'd pass the test he'd laid out for her. "We're working on getting him down now, but it's going to take some time."

"Getting him down? From where?" She glanced at Mac. "Where did he..." The words *hang himself* stuck on the back of her tongue like peanut butter, and her next breath shuddered against her ribs. "Where exactly is he?"

Special Agent Watters tilted his head to the side with a small smirk. "He's all the way up, Chief. Six stories, dangling from one of the shakeout hooks on the personnel chute side. Where else would he be in there?" Some sort of twisted pleasure tinted the words, almost like he enjoyed shocking her.

Or he wanted to judge her response.

She didn't know what he expected, but the response he got leaned more toward disbelief than horror. There was no way... "How?" The single word rocketed from her mouth and bounced off the walls around her.

Mac, hovering behind her left shoulder, muttered, "That's what I said."

The agent's face registered no reaction as he stepped away from the door and swung his arm toward the entrance. "See for yourself, though I have to ask you to stay on this side to do so."

An invisible wall went up between Cassidy and the threshold. She couldn't step past it to look. *God, you have to do this. I can't.* Death in a war zone was one thing. Death at home held a special place of horror, reinforcing the fact that nowhere in the world could offer true safety. Cassidy took the last step forward, and a blast of air smacked against her face. She squeezed her eyes shut for a second, wishing she could peek through her fingers like she used to do when her father watched *Twilight Zone* reruns. If she could survey the scene one finger at a time, maybe it wouldn't be as bad as her brain wanted her to believe. With strength she knew didn't come from her, she opened her eyes and looked up.

Boots. For the rest of her life, she'd see those boots, dangling where they shouldn't be, swaying with the current of the drying fans that blew air from beneath the grated floor. She couldn't look at his face. Couldn't let it brand itself in her mind and haunt her every night for the rest of her life.

But something was wrong. She tore her gaze from Private Anderson's boots and surveyed the room, piecing together what had happened. "He couldn't have," she said, her voice so low she knew no one else could hear it.

As the analytical side of her mind beat back her emotions, her voice grew firmer. Thoughts that should have stayed in her head rushed from her mouth in a torrent. "To hang himself he'd have to, I don't know, have twenty-foot-long arms." With the controls to raise the chutes six stories on one side of the building, there was no way for Anderson to noose himself and still reach them. She looked over her shoulder at Mac for confirmation.

His jaw set harder than she'd ever seen it. When he caught her watching him, his eyebrows drew together. "She's right. He'd have to be David Copperfield to pull that off."

Cassidy turned to Special Agent Watters. The way the man worked his mouth spoke volumes. He either typically smoked or chewed toothpicks or—

she let her eyes wander to his bald head—lollipops. The irrational giggle bubbled again. She was losing control.

He lasered in on Cassidy. "He call you tonight? Text you? Any missed calls or strange messages?"

It was a good thing Mac had warned her. Such a left-field question would have stunned her speechless otherwise. Pulling her BlackBerry from her triceps pocket, she glanced at the screen and handed it over. "No. Nothing."

"You have a home phone? And can I look through this one?" At her nod, Watters punched buttons and scrolled through a few menus.

"Just the cell. Why?" Yeah, she knew, but she wanted to hear him say it. When she was a little girl, her grandmother used to collect butterflies and pin them into picture frames. Something about Watters made her feel like one of those butterflies. She needed some sense of control, some way to guide the conversation, before she peeked at Anderson again and her insides flew apart. With a step backward, she walked to the outside door and looked across the parking lot at her soldiers. The group had grown larger. She had to hold it together for them... And maybe even for her freedom.

Special Agent Watters thrust her BlackBerry under her nose, jerking Cassidy into the conversation as she stepped away from the door. "You're right. Nothing there."

And no apology for violating my privacy either. Nice. She snatched the phone and shoved it into her pocket, grateful for any small action that gave her forward momentum.

"You're right, by the way." Watters shrugged and put his hand to his mouth, looked bewildered when it came up empty, then refocused on Cassidy and Mac. "We don't think he did this to himself, although it might be a bungled attempt to make it look like he did."

Murder. The unspoken word froze Cassidy's emotions and thoughts into lumps of solid, unyielding ice, so numb she pinched her arm to make sure she was still alive.

"We'll need accountability of every key to this building. Our suspect list starts there."

Realization slid down her spine as she reached into her pocket for her key ring. Only a handful of people had after-hours access to this building.

And she was one of them.

Shane gripped the side of the truck bed, braced his feet against the tire and leaned back, tight muscles stretching across his shoulders. He rolled his neck from side to side and tried to keep from looking at the door to the rigger shed for the seventy-fifth time in half an hour. What was going on in there?

He should have gone with Cassy. Should have insisted on escorting her, even though the master sergeant had met her at the door. If Jackson was telling the truth about Cassy being the suspected drug smuggler, would they assume she had something to do with Anderson's death, too? Not knowing how she was doing, what was going on or how bad the situation was was worse than facing down a gang of armed terrorists.

He'd never been afraid during firefights in the streets. It was enemies he couldn't see who got to him, the ones who hid in the bushes, concealed themselves on rooftops, looked like every other civilian before they went violent and blew a few guys away without warning. Those were the enemies he hated to come up against. Those were the enemies who still woke him at night in a cold sweat, even in his own bed in the safety of his own apartment. What you didn't see could get you killed.

Pulling himself to center, Shane let go of the sides of the truck, brushed his hands together and resumed pacing up and down the white line of the parking space, not caring that he looked like a driver acing the sobriety test.

Yeah, what you don't see can get you killed, and he couldn't see one single enemy who fired rounds at Cassy. Someone broke into her house and tried to drag her into the night. Someone tampered with her computer. Someone stole papers from her desk. Someone rigged the inventories to her shipping containers. His best hunch turned out to be a federal agent, and the only other suspect was dead.

Shane clenched his jaw. He'd give up every penny of the combat pay from his last tour if this was really a suicide. It was too convenient.

Not a shadow moved in the parking lot. Even the soldiers had dispersed, probably gathered in barrack rooms and conjecturing about the whos and whats of this surreal morning. Shane had no idea what he expected to see, but it sure would be nice if God cracked open the heavens and rained an answer down on his head right about now. Too bad there wasn't a cloud in the sky.

A familiar black BMW screeched into the parking lot and dragged to a crooked halt in the space beside Shane's. *Great.*

Jackson burst out of the car, dressed in jeans and a blue striped polo, and slammed the door behind him with a dull thud. When he spotted Shane, he froze in midstride, eyes widening, then narrowing faster than Shane could blink.

Shane stood straighter and squared off, fists balled by his thighs. It didn't matter what the guy did for a living or why he was in Cassy's life, but Shane couldn't take any more of him. He'd never spoken two words to Jackson before, but the very air the man breathed rode his last nerve. "You need something?"

It took Jackson a second to locate his speaking

ability, but he found it as he stepped toward the building. "I need to find Chief Matthews."

So he could arrest her? Harass her? Twist the knife he'd stuck in her back? "No."

The utterance stopped Jackson's progress as effectively as a blow to the spine. He pivoted in mid-turn and tilted his head as he eyed Shane. "What did you say?"

"I believe it was *no*."

Jackson blinked twice, then the corner of his lip drew into a smirk. "Who are you again?"

"Nobody you need to worry about." Shane couldn't stand the look on the guy's face. So smug. So arrogant. So something Shane couldn't read but didn't like anyway. "Unless you want me to be somebody you have to worry about. And I don't think you do."

"Really." With the word, Jackson stuck his chest out in dominant defiance. For someone who was supposed to be emotionally disinterested, he acted like he had a vested interest in Cassy. Or was it just for show?

Shane shook his head. Was the dude really going to bow up on him now? "Do I know you?"

Jackson glanced to his right and faltered for an instant so short that Shane almost didn't catch it. "Doubtful, but I know you. You're the low-life who cheated on Cassidy. Shane Logan, right?" He closed the gap between them until they were toe-to-toe, two boxers on the mat squaring off for the title bout.

And Cassy was the prize.

Shane ran his tongue along the back of his teeth. This was juvenile, and he'd graduated from high school sixteen years ago. He refused to humiliate Cassy by brawling in the parking lot with a smug punk like Jackson. Shoving his hands in his pockets, Shane leaned against the truck, propped his foot on the tire behind him and waited. More than he wanted to breathe, he wanted to ask the guy why he was so interested if he was only surveilling Cassy, but that was a conversation that didn't need to happen here.

The lack of response flipped a switch in Jackson's personality. A string of curses fogged the air around them. Another time and another place and the man probably would have spat on Shane's feet right there.

Jackson wanted him to react, but he'd have to keep wanting. Shane wouldn't be goaded into planting a fist square in the guy's nose, even though his muscles begged to let fly. He fell back on training to take the edge off his fight response. Although still guarded, Shane relaxed his stance and tried to drag the disdain from his face. "A man is dead. Out of respect for him and for Cassy, I think you need to bring it down a notch and remember where you are."

Every ounce of the thin veneer of cool Jackson wore dropped away. His face grew redder than a desert sunrise. "Who do you think you are?"

The roar bounced off the nearby buildings and hit Shane's ears twice. He fought a wince and just did manage to hold on to his composure. "The better question might be who are *you?*"

"Answer me. Tell me, before I—"

"Before you do what?" Cassy's voice cut through the night like a bayonet. "Before you make an even bigger scene? Or before the MPs come out here to find out what's going on?"

Jackson took a giant step back, his eyes hanging on to Shane's in fury for a second before he turned.

This was going to be good. Cassy had held her emotions in check when she found out Jackson wasn't who he said he was. As much as his heart ached for her, Shane couldn't resist watching this guy get what he deserved. He hoped it involved a fist to the jaw. Shane crossed his arms over his chest and settled in to watch. No way was he going to miss this.

One glimpse of Cassy's face yanked his spine straight. Her expression was drawn tight, her eyes swollen with tears he knew she refused to shed in front of anybody, if ever. Shane had seen that look of devastation on her face only a few times before, and it still woke him at night. This time he could do something about it. She needed him, needed somebody to tell her it would be okay if she let go. He dropped his arms to his side, aiming to go straight to her.

But Jackson stood between them. "Cassidy, I heard what happened and—"

Cassy's hand, palm mere centimeters from his nose, deflected the words. "Know what, Jackson? I'm not in the mood. And you don't really care anyway."

"But, I—"

"You." She pointed at Jackson's expensive ride. "Go. Home. Unless you're here to arrest me for something, leave me alone."

Shane bit back a smile.

Jackson moved to say something else, but Cassy stepped around him and narrowed her eyes at Shane. "And you, take me home."

The look of shock on Jackson's face should have filled Shane with triumph, but it didn't. Something in Cassy's expression was off. The light in her eyes looked more like concealed fury than warm favoritism.

Muttering under his breath, Jackson acted like he might square off against Shane again, but he dropped his shoulders and skulked around the front of his car. Just before he slammed the door, Shane could have sworn he heard, "This isn't over."

He rolled his eyes. This had to be a joke. The guy was like the worst cartoon villain ever invented. All he needed was a mustache to twirl.

Shane didn't move until Jackson's car exited the parking lot in a spray of gravel. *And don't come back now, ya hear?* He allowed himself the smirk he'd been holding in for the past few minutes. It felt good.

His amusement fell to his toes when he glanced at Cassy. The ground almost trembled under her feet as she stalked around to the passenger side of the truck and yanked the door open.

Uh-oh. He'd seen this before. Cautiously, he pulled his truck door open and rested a foot on the running board. Instead of grieving she was about to—

"What in the world were you thinking?"

If he wasn't careful, her gaze would burn holes clean through his head.

"Have you lost your mind, throwing down like a teenager in my parking lot? Were you trying to humiliate me? Don't you have any respect? For me or for Anderson? Why on earth—"

"It wasn't me." Shane's voice, low and flat, filled the truck. He punctuated the statement with a period by easing his truck door shut instead of slamming it in exclamation.

She huffed and crossed her arms over her chest, looking exactly like his two-year-old niece in full pout. "You're going to tell me the two of you weren't about to come to blows out there?"

"No. But if there had been blows, it would have been your secret agent friend throwin' 'em." He gripped the steering wheel and channeled his frustration into the vinyl. "Buckle your seat belt."

"He's not my friend."

"Good to know. Now buckle up."

When her seat belt clicked, Shane popped the truck into Reverse and aimed for her house. It'd be a chilly ride if she didn't get those arms uncrossed soon. He studied her when they pulled up to a stoplight. Her eyes were fixed straight out the windshield, focused on anything but him. What was the old saying? One step forward, two steps back? Propping his forearm on the steering wheel, he said, "Do you really think I'd—"

"Yes."

Well. That answered that question. "I wouldn't have hit him."

"Maybe. Maybe not. Because he didn't hit you first, we'll never know." Cassy didn't even look at him. "Are you going to sit at this intersection until I can just turn around and walk back to PT in the morning, or are you going to take me home so I can grab a few hours of sleep?"

"You and I both know that's not going to happen." Shane eased off the brake and pulled through the intersection, then turned onto Reilly Road.

"What's that mean?"

"You'll lay awake all night and stare at the ceiling." He flicked his lights at an oncoming car to signal them to dim their high beams. "You forget I know you. Right now, you're busy digging a hole to bury your emotions so they can't rise out of the grave and attack you later."

"You *knew* me. Don't go making assumptions about who I am now." When he glanced at her, she'd turned her head to stare out the side window. Apparently, they were in the two-steps-back portion of this discussion. "And I'm not. There's a difference between burying and processing. Now stop talking to me so I can process."

What was he doing here? Even as she fought to bury her emotions, he found himself drawn in more. And the longer he stayed close to her, the more he wanted to find the road that led to what they used to be.

No, not what they used to be. What they were now. This more mature Cassy was not the same girl who'd left him with a broken heart. She was stronger than that. She was almost too strong.

Shane gripped the steering wheel tighter. She tried too hard to do it all alone. And even though he hadn't done anything wrong, had never been unfaithful to her, he felt responsible for the walls she hid behind. He should have tried harder to prove his innocence, should have gone and searched out what made her suspect infidelity in the first place. Instead, in his anger at her lack of trust, he'd rolled over and let everything they had die.

Right now, more than anything, Shane wanted to pull the truck over, unbuckle both of their seat belts, pull her close and give her a shoulder to cry on. But in a million years she'd never shed a tear in front of him. She'd been the same way all those years ago, and it appeared nothing had changed. Emotions were better buried than felt, better hidden than seen. Angry outbursts were better than tears. Sometimes he swore he was more of a girl than she was when it came to emotions—not that he'd ever say that out loud.

By the time Shane pulled into her driveway and turned off the truck, the air between them in the cab was at least twenty degrees colder than the predawn air outside. Cassy hadn't said another word the entire twenty-minute drive home. Now she turned and held out her hand, palm up. "Keys?"

"What?"

"You locked the house. Give me the keys."

Shane stared hard out the front window, trying to think of a way to stall her. The last thing he wanted was for her to go into a dark house to fight these demons alone. Whether she needed to blow up angry or dissolve in tears, she needed to do something other than build yet another wall around her already fortified emotions.

A slow smile tweaked one corner of his mouth, and he tipped his head toward the windshield. Yes, it was juvenile, but he was desperate. "Is that a basketball goal over your garage?"

"Yes."

"Yours?"

"No. The landlord put it up for his son before they moved. Can I have the keys?"

"You had the best free throw in our entire high school, and you're going to tell me you never once threw a ball at that hoop?" He knew she had. From the beginning of their friendship and all the way through their marriage, whenever she got mad, she spent hours in the driveway, lobbing shot after shot until she'd unknotted all of the world's problems. "Where's the ball, Cassy?" Shane threw the gear into Neutral and let the truck roll backward down the slight incline toward the end of the driveway before shifting into Park.

"What are you doing? It's three in the morning. You're going to shoot baskets now? The neighbors will kill you. Be my guest, but I'm going to bed. Ball's in the side yard by the trash can, last I saw it."

"And the last you told me, the neighbors on one side of you are on vacation, and the house on the other side's been vacant for months." Shane popped the door open and put one foot on the ground, propping the other on the running board. He dropped his gaze straight to her eyes. "Actually, I'm not going to shoot anything. But you're going to play me for the keys, just like you used to play me over who was going to do the dishes."

"Wh—"

He slammed the door on her protest and headed for the side yard without looking back.

Cassidy blinked as the door sliced off her protest. The boy had lost his fool mind if he thought she was going to play pickup basketball in her driveway at oh-dark-thirty on this night of all nights. She'd sleep in the truck before she caved to such a request. Determined to keep the upper hand even as she felt herself losing ground, Cassidy crossed her arms, leaned her head against the seat and closed her eyes. The *thunk* of a basketball hitting cement twanged against her eardrum, but she refused to look up.

After a minute or so, silence reigned. Good. He'd given up. As she moved for a one-eyed peek, a dull thud blew through the cab of the truck. She scrambled up in time to see Shane catch the ball he'd bounced off the windshield. The twist of his mouth said he stifled a laugh at her reaction.

This had gone far enough. After the night she'd had, the last thing she needed was his regressing to high school all over her driveway. Leaping out of the truck, she slammed the door just in time to catch his chest pass, which drove her a step back. Her planned argument died before it ever reached the air as the amusement she'd seen earlier had been replaced with a challenge.

Without thinking, Cassidy lobbed the ball in a perfect arc from where she stood at the door of the truck. It *whooshed* through the net with a sound like falling snowflakes. "Now, give me my keys and give up this stupidity."

Shane slowly bounced the ball and studied her. "You beat me to five and I'll give you the keys."

"Shane, I—" She caught the ball instead of finishing her sentence. The familiar scrub of dusty leather against her hand twined with the sight of the man in front of her. The horrors Cassy had seen tonight disappeared into a haze that muddled past and present, this driveway with another from long ago. One where they often battled one-on-one until the game and the man playing it drove all the ugliness from her thoughts. She bounced the ball once and pressed it between her palms. It wouldn't work tonight. The time for playing games was long past.

"Play." The commanding arrogance in that one word bounced off the trees.

Something in her snapped, and she drove hard, spun around him and sank the shot. Whirling on him, she hurled the rebound at his head. If he wanted to play games, she'd make him fight for every moment of her time.

He caught the ball neatly, then watched her for a second. Instead of rushing forward like he always had in the past, Shane merely shot the ball and sank it. "I'm within a point of you. You'd better hustle, Matthews."

The calm evenness of his voice stoked the fire

in her chest. Retrieving the ball, she fired it at the goal and watched it bounce off the rim straight into Shane's waiting hands. As he leaped for a shot, she brought her hand down to knock the ball away but missed. Her left hand drove into a glancing blow on his shoulder that forced her ring finger back with a *pop*. Pain rocketed up her arm as her shoulder crashed into Shane's chest and sent them both sprawling onto the grass beside the driveway.

Rolling away from Shane onto her side, Cassy cradled her hand, the pain dragging tears from her eyes. When the first one rolled down her cheek, it opened the invitation to all of the ones behind it, and she buried her face in the grass and sobbed, wishing Shane would disappear and the world would leave her alone.

It wasn't fair. Anderson was dead. She choked on sorrow and horror at the sight etched into her memory. He was just a kid. And they probably thought she did it. Somebody out there already had her pegged as a traitor. Might as well call her a murderer, too.

She'd never missed her father so much. His quick legal mind would have known what to do, would have known how to defend her, how to get her out of this. He'd have poured her his own lemonade, sat down and pored over case law and made the whole world right again. It wasn't fair. It wasn't fair for

God to take away one of the only people who had always believed in her, no matter what.

There was silence outside of her tears. Maybe Shane had left. Maybe this much emotion was too much for him. Her chest tightened, and the sobs racked harder. She didn't want him to leave. She needed him. The truth solidified the pain of tears at the base of her throat. As much as she wanted to be able to do everything on her own, she couldn't. He was right to ask her who she trusted. He'd asked for her trust so he could help her. She should have listened all along. Maybe if she had, her life would be different... And Private Anderson would still be alive.

A soft rustle, and Shane's hand rested between her shoulder blades. "Cassy?"

She shook her head, fresh tears exhausting her. "All I could see was boots. Up there, over my head. Boots. Where they...never should...have been." The words tumbled out with the sobs. "And all I could think was... One more. On my watch. One more. Right in front of me."

Shane sighed and continued to trail his fingers up her back, telegraphing cold chills that eventually overrode her tears. Part of her wanted to crawl into his arms and let him soothe the horrible image and the guilt away, but the other part remembered what happened the last time she let him hold her. She didn't need to go there again, not if he couldn't reciprocate.

Swallowing hard, Cassidy rolled onto her back and stared at the dark sky, where the stars shone so faintly she could barely make them out. "I miss my dad." She swiped at her face with the sleeve of her ACU top.

"So do I." Shane stretched out beside her and stared up at the sky. He sniffed. "I was thinking on the way over here... He'd have known what to do and who to talk to. He was a lot smarter than me. A lot more..." His shrug rustled against the dry summer grass. "Did your mom ever tell you I came to his funeral?"

The question brought every spinning thought in her head to a halt. "What?" It was a whisper he shouldn't have been able to hear. "But...you were in North Africa."

"I arranged some things. Probably some things I shouldn't have gotten away with arranging. But when your mom got word to me, I thought you might need me. Then when I got here and saw you, I couldn't do that to you. You were so angry the last time we talked and so devastated at the funeral. It just... I sat at the back."

"I wish I'd known." Some part of her had wanted him there, even though she hadn't seen him in five years. The ache as she sat there and stared at the casket was as much for her best friend as it was for her father. Maybe it would have changed everything if she'd known.

Shane propped up on one elbow, his hand brushing her arm. "How did you know where I was on assignment?"

Cassidy shrugged and kept her eyes on the sky. This conversation was loaded, and her finger was on the trigger. She just wasn't sure if she was ready for the recoil if she fired. Now would be a good time to move away enough to break his touch, but something deep inside tied her to that slight connection. "So your little basketball game. You knew I'd cry if you made me mad."

"Know what?" Shane sat straighter and rested his forearms on his bent knees, looking down at her. "Before you were a soldier, you were a girl."

"I was?" In spite of everything, it was hard to keep a trace of amusement from her voice.

"You are. A woman. A female. A human being. You don't cease to be who you are just because you become a soldier, no matter what they drum into and out of you at basic training and at Warrant Officer Candidate School. Your soldiers respect you because you command respect, not because you're male or female. You drive back your emotions like you think it's weakness to show them. It's not. It's healthy. You'll come unglued if you keep this up."

The proclamation struck her heart before it reached her head. "I don't know. It's a habit."

"A bad one. It's possible to be too strong, Cassy." He reached for her. "Now, stop cradling your hand and acting like you didn't hurt it. Let me take a look."

"I'm fine." Even as she said it, she heard the very attitude Shane was warning her against. "It's not broken," she muttered in a last weak act of defiance. Not that it mattered. Somewhere between his defending her from Jackson in the parking lot and proclaiming her strength as her weakness, Cassidy had surrendered more than her injured hand.

Shane took her hand in his and inspected her ring finger in the light from the streetlamp. "It's not even bruised." He laid a light kiss on her knuckle.

The warmth of the touch rushed through her fingers and up her arm, thawing the last frozen corner of her heart. Everything else might be spinning out of control, but this... This was a safe place in the crazy storm swirling around her. She pressed her lips together and raised her head to meet his eyes. He was too close, much too close. He was bound to be able to feel the heat torching her cheeks. And as she watched him, she caught the exact moment he read her reaction to him. The edges of his eyes softened, his lids dipping ever so slightly. His breath grew as shallow as hers, and his grip on her fingers tightened.

She couldn't get enough of his face. In the grip of

whatever this emotion was, she couldn't stop staring at him, studying his eyes, his cheeks…his lips. "I need you." Her words were a breath between them, so silent he could only have heard them if he was listening with his heart.

The words didn't seem to register, or if they did, he ignored them. Tugging lightly at her wrist, his eyes never leaving her hand, he pulled her up until her head bent next to his. "Did you know you have an indentation right here?" His index finger traced a lazy circle around the base of her ring finger, his voice husky and low.

"It… It won't go away."

"Maybe there's a reason for that?" For the first time, he caught her eyes in his gaze. "Maybe because our marriage was the truth and our divorce was the lie?"

"You left without a fight." The words were a mumble of sound and emotion. It was her last argument, voiced out of habit, and feeble even to her own ears.

A smile quirked the corner of his mouth as his voice fell lower. "Are you really still angry about that?"

It was hard to push the words out past the renewed lump in her throat. "Not really."

His grin flashed with full force before he closed the gap between them and pressed a kiss to her forehead. Slipping his cheek against her temple, he whispered into her hair, "Do I have to tell you I'm pretty sure I never quit loving you?"

Before she could respond, his lips found hers and wiped away the last of her doubts.

FOURTEEN

The sun barely peeped over the edge of the world when Cassidy shifted her Trailblazer into Park at the rigger shed. For the second time in a handful of days, she considered a nap right there in the front seat. She'd spent the past few hours sitting on the porch steps with Shane, alternately crying out emotions she'd folded inside for years and reveling in the joy of finding him again. For the first time in her memory, Cassidy felt like hope existed.

Still, while last night's freefall had been relatively smooth, the scene outside the rigger shed was a hard landing in reality.

It was rare for the company to be hopping at 0530, but the parking lot was near capacity, and her soldiers already milled about. One young private, when he spotted her Trailblazer, bolted inside like he was on a mission. Either word of Anderson's death had kept them all awake or morbid curiosity had drawn them here to see what they could see. Human nature being what it was, the answer was probably closer to both. She'd seen one too many soldiers after a buddy's death, repulsed and drawn in all at the same time, battling anger and guilt for wanting to know all of the details.

Cassidy grabbed her messenger bag and made it halfway to the door before Colonel Fryar stepped out and settled his maroon beret over his graying hair, clearly intent on intercepting her. His dark eyes had a look in them that she'd only seen when a dressing down was in order. That look had never been leveled on her before.

Surely he was upset about Anderson, but his expression spoke of anger aimed straight at her. She swallowed hard and dug deep for her command stance as she saluted and recited the Eighty-Second Airborne motto. "All the Way, sir."

"Airborne, Chief." He popped a quick return salute and dipped his head toward the far side of the parking lot, where empty shipping containers stood like discarded toy trains. "Walk with me."

Cassidy hiked her bag higher on her shoulder and fell into step with the colonel. A thousand questions fought to rush out of her mouth, but she bit her lower lip to stem the tide. He'd speak when he was ready, and she wasn't about to increase his ire by rushing him.

They were out of earshot of the soldiers near the door before he said anything. "They're emptying your office, Matthews."

Cassidy stumbled to a stop and gaped at Colonel Fryar's back. "My…" She turned to the building. "My what?"

Before she could take a step, the colonel gripped her elbow. "Tell me what's going on."

Jerking her arm free, Cassidy whirled to her superior, barely holding her emotions in check. "Sir, you tell me. Exactly who is emptying my office? Have I been relieved? Because of Anderson? Because we were missing a container? What?" Cold fear slapped her face and sent shivers to her toes. Jackson. He'd sold her soul.

She should have let the fight between Shane and him run its natural course last night. At least there would have been some punishment for him this morning.

"Chief, as far as I'm concerned, this job is still yours. I just don't know how CID is going to feel about it."

Her brain raced so fast that it fogged her hearing. There was no way she'd heard right. "Criminal Investigation?" Sooner or later, she'd have to stop asking questions and come up with a statement or two. "Is this about Private Anderson?"

"Among other things." Colonel Fryar's gaze softened. For the first time since this surreal encounter started, Cassidy realized his anger was directed at whatever was going on inside the building and not at her. "I hope you have an alibi for last night."

Her mind raced as her stomach turned to solid lead, and her composure faltered. "An—an alibi? For what?" Her bag slid from her shoulder into the dust at her feet. "I was right. They think I…" Nausea threatened to stem her words, but she swallowed twice, and her voice dropped to a whisper. "They think I killed him. Why would they think I'd do such a thing?"

"It gets worse."

Spots danced before Cassidy's eyes. She could not—would not—pass out in the middle of a parking lot with accusations like these thundering over her head. "I'm sure it does."

"They went straight for your computers and secured them before they went anywhere else. And chances are high you're going to see a search warrant for your house within the hour."

"Looking for?" The question was automatic. She already knew.

"Somebody's been smuggling drugs into the country using our supply lines. It's been a problem in a few of the supply units, but now they've tried to establish an arm using the parachutes we bring back over. We never had a missing container. CID confiscated it at New Cumberland. It was loaded. The bulk of the parachute bags were padded with heroin. A few contractors at the shipyard in Afghanistan have been brought in. Looks like the ringleader paid off soldiers on this end to unload the containers and turn his stash over to him."

Cassidy closed her eyes. Even though some small corner of her mind had held on to denial, the truth could no longer be silenced. One—or more—of her soldiers had a part in bringing drugs into the country. In her equipment. And she'd stake her career on one of them being Anderson's killer. Her first urge was to turn and study the men and women milling around the parking lot, but she just couldn't do it. She still couldn't look at her soldiers and think one of them could do something so heinous. "Anderson. He switched lockup to be here on Thursday night after the shipping containers come in. It would have been the hand-off." She met the colonel's eye again.

He arched an eyebrow. "You knew?"

"I suspected." With as few sentences as possible, she outlined her week and dumped all the information she had, no matter how circumstantial.

"You didn't call the police the very first time someone broke into your house? Were you thinking straight, Matthews?"

She nodded. Yes, it had made sense at the time, but in hindsight it was a major lapse in judgment. Especially now.

"Alibi?"

"Yes, sir. Fortunately." Cassidy inhaled deeply and thanked God Shane had talked her into going to church last night. It hadn't seemed like the greatest idea at the time, but it just might save her career—and maybe her life—now. "I was with a friend. At church. We got in around 2230 or somewhere in there."

Colonel Fryar puffed his cheeks and exhaled loudly. "Ten-thirty. They think Anderson died before that. Good to know."

"But you haven't answered the question of why they're looking at me." Cassidy clasped her hands behind her back to stop their shaking. Murder... Drugs... Smuggling... Her home violated... Her office trashed by investigators...

"My guess?" The older man turned and started a slow walk to the building. "You're the one here day in and day out with these guys. They're looking at you first because you're supposed to know everything that goes on here. You're the subject matter expert when it comes to packing and shipping this equipment. You're the logical first target. But they won't find a thing on your computers, and your alibi will clear you for last night. You're safe."

Cassidy stepped around a pothole. "That doesn't change the fact somebody in this unit murdered Anderson."

"You're sure he was in on it?"

"Fairly sure. A couple of the guys have mentioned he's been throwing money around. And he did act weird about a lot of things, but he also said there was a new girl in his life, so I initially wrote it off as that. I do know he stopped me in the parking lot yesterday afternoon and wanted to talk to me. When somebody else showed up, he clammed up and said it could wait. I think he wanted to talk and somebody didn't want him to."

"Who showed up?" The colonel stopped and turned to look down at her.

Cassidy hesitated. She wasn't sure what to say. Jackson had warned her against blowing his cover any further. "He's a contractor. Jackson Reese."

"Hmm. Might be worth mentioning."

Cassidy started to take another step, then stopped, dread tensing her muscles. "The emails. My computers. Somebody tampered with my computer at home and tried to access the one here. Anderson supposedly fixed the problem, but…Colonel, what happens if they dig up what they're looking for and it's not mine?"

"Then you'd better hope we figure out who really did this before they find anything to implicate you."

The warm breath of a morning breeze brushed by Shane as he ran, chilling his skin and tugging at the edges of his T-shirt. It wasn't too hot out yet, but it was definitely too muggy for the pace he'd set. His lungs felt like he'd pulled off his damp shirt and inhaled it, but he pushed on. The breeze might be cooling his body, but it wasn't doing much to take the heat from his gut.

He'd set feet to pavement as soon as Cassidy left for work, too keyed up to sleep. Nothing he'd imagined had prepared him for her words last night, for the idea that she was truly willing to try again. As long as they sat together on her porch, she was safe. But the instant she left the circle of his protection…

Shane had hoped familiar activity would clear his mind and give him time to think and pray. So far, all it had done was raise his temperature and increase his frustration. Where were those magic endorphins he needed? *Come on, kick in and drag some clarity with you.*

He couldn't figure out how much danger Cassy faced. So far she'd managed to dodge their blows, but they sure had dug their fingers in all around her. And according to Derek—who still had a network of connections Shane envied—word had it Private Anderson's death was anything but a suicide.

Shane's pace picked up. He'd suspected it, but with all of the talking they'd done this morning, Cassy hadn't bothered to tell him. He couldn't wait to corner her and find out why. If they were going to puzzle this thing out, she had to trust him, and it seemed some small part of her still didn't.

Shane stumbled, and momentum made it a fight to keep himself from hurtling headfirst into the white line on the pavement. Whoa. Too fast. This was a jog, not a sprint. Big difference.

He glanced around and realized the surroundings

had taken a drastic change from when he'd first left the house. The pavement had narrowed from the well-traveled two-lane on the edge of Cassy's neighborhood and become a back country road, barely wide enough for two cars to pass without scraping doors. Pine trees rose tall around him, needles whispering in the breeze.

Slowing, Shane turned and walked backward, studying where he'd been. He glanced at his watch. Forty-five minutes and no way to determine his pace. There was no telling how far he'd come. He smirked wryly and hoped he hadn't made any turns on the way. Otherwise, he'd never figure out where he was.

Now that he'd taken it down, the last thing his legs and lungs wanted was to exert themselves again, but he forced himself into a jog and pushed on. He had to go back to the rigger shed and pull more surveillance. The reason he didn't know anything was, well, he didn't know anything. He needed to lay eyes on the people who worked for her and figure out who might be capable of smuggling…and murder.

Just as he fell into an easy rhythm, the cell phone at his hip rang. He grimaced and slowed his pace once more. It would be an even bigger fight to get going again now. This had better be good.

Cassy's number flashed on the screen. Yeah, that was a good enough reason to take a breather. He stopped, pressed a button and jerked the phone to his ear. "You miss me already?"

"Where are you?"

Shane swiped at sweat that threatened to drip into his eye. "Top o' the mornin' to you, too, missy."

"Stop it. Are you anywhere near my house right now?"

Concern knotted at the base of his spine. Her voice stretched thin over the connection, low and desperate. "What's going on? I'm close to an hour away. On foot."

"Then I need Derek's number. And how are you an hour away?"

"Running. Slow down and tell me what you need and I'll figure out a way to take care of it."

Her sigh was loud in his ear. "Anderson was murdered. And now CID is here emptying my office. The colonel says my house is probably next."

"Do they think you—"

"I think so, but they're after my computers first and foremost. I left the backup of my desktop at the house. Shane, I need you to get back to the house and email the contents of it to yourself. I want to know what they have. I have a bad feeling I'm about to be set up, and it's all got to do with those emails and the hardware switch Derek found."

His brain stuck on the *I need you* and shot lightning to his scalp. It was doubtful he'd ever get tired of hearing that. He shook it off and started walking, grasping for the rest of the sentence before he could answer. "Hard drive. Got it. Where is it?"

"It's in the office closet, in the pocket of my dress blues. Shane… Hurry." She killed the call.

Shane gripped the phone tighter and fought a string of words he hadn't uttered in years. Helplessness like he'd never known washed over him. There was nothing he could do from here. It would take forever to run to her house, and he didn't even know where he was to call Derek to come get him. He couldn't exactly say, "I think I'm on the same road I started out on, but I just can't be sure." *God, I could really use a hand right now.*

Setting his feet on the road, Shane pushed toward Cassy's, alternately praying and puzzling out how to handle her request. She'd wanted to call Derek, but Shane feared dragging his buddy into something when he had only a vague idea what was going on. What would happen if the authorities got to the house and found Derek digging through her closet? Then again, what would happen if they got there and found *him?*

Sunlight glinted on a metallic object about a quarter of a mile ahead, and Shane picked up the pace. A road sign. *Thank you, Jesus.* Derek could find him, and hopefully they'd be able to do as Cassy asked.

Although he'd never imagined having to pull a recon mission at his ex-wife's house.

FIFTEEN

Cassidy sank into her chair and surveyed her office. A rectangle of clean tile revealed where her computer used to sit. Despite the colonel's warning, they hadn't exactly torn the place apart. All that was missing was her desktop computer and her work laptop, and it was certain they'd hit her house next. Someone had flipped through the papers on her desk, but it didn't look like the action was more than a halfhearted bit of idle curiosity. Whatever questions the investigators had about her, it was clear they believed her computers held the answers.

She gave a quick glance at the closed office door, then dropped her head into her hands. All she wanted was to curl into a ball under her desk and cry. Blast Shane for opening the floodgates to all of her emotions last night. Tears hadn't slid down her cheeks since their divorce was finalized, and now they couldn't seem to stop. Every wall she'd built around her heart cracked under the pressure. She balled her fists and pressed them tightly to her eyes. *Soldiers don't cry, no matter what Shane says.*

A light tap at the door brought her head up. She swallowed the tears battering the back of her throat and took a deep breath. "Come in."

McIntyre slipped in and shut the door behind him. "Doin' okay in here? You look like somebody died."

The slightest sting of disappointment pricked the ache at the back of her throat. Where was Shane? "Somebody did die, Mac." Cassidy sat back and laid her fingertips on the edge of her desk. "And Colonel Fryar ordered me to go home for the rest of the day."

"Poor choice of words. And you're still here." He dipped his head toward the chair in front of her desk, and she nodded her consent. Mac sat, crossed his legs and hung his beret on his knee. "The entire company is talking."

"I'm sure. How many are convinced I'm a murderer?"

"You'd be surprised."

Cassidy looked up from her fingertips. "That many? Really? After all this time, that many assume I'd—"

"None."

"Not even one?" The tears she'd carefully corked squeezed past the barrier and leaked into her eyes. She pressed her fingertips against her lower lids and tried to force them back in. *Crybaby.*

"You're a tough leader, but you've always been

honest with them. Not a one of them believes you could have strung up Anderson. The problem is they're starting to point fingers at each other in some pretty subtle ways, asking what everybody was up to last night, where they were when they found out, who they think is behind it. If we don't do something soon, it's going to be brother against brother. It'd be physically impossible for him to hang himself that way, and every rigger out there knows it."

"I can't stand to think one of them did it." Cassidy dropped her hands into her lap and stared at her fingernails. She'd never been in a battle position surrounded by enemies, but it must feel something like this.

Mac didn't say anything for a long time, and the silence stretched almost to breaking.

Cassidy opened her mouth to speak when a sharp rap on the door grabbed both of their attention.

After a quick glance at a shrugging Mac, Cassidy called for the person to enter.

Shane stepped into the room. He must have brought every bit of oxygen from the outside world in with him because Cassidy took her first deep breath of the day. She should have known he wouldn't leave her to fight this battle alone, and she hadn't realized how isolated she felt until he walked in.

His eyes met hers, and she felt the tingle of relief in her fingers and toes, then sat back hard in her chair, her eyes glued to his.

Mac stood, blocking her view of Shane. She wanted to lean to the side and find those eyes again, to regain the connection that crackled between them. It was the one thing that made her feel like she might come out of this with some part of her life intact.

"I'm sorry, sir. Did you need something?" Mac's back was rigid.

He was trying to protect her. Amusement over-rode the heat of Shane's presence, and she stepped around the desk, finding Shane's eyes again and refusing to break contact. With a hand on Mac's shoulder she said, "It's okay, Mac. I asked him to come back in."

Mac visibly relaxed, and Cassidy dropped her hand from his shoulder. The two men gave brief greetings before Shane looked at Cassidy. "Can we..." He glanced at Mac. "I need to talk to you alone, if that's okay."

The look in his eye told Cassidy more bad news was headed her way. She swallowed hard. All she wanted was to run into his arms and hide, but army regulation wouldn't let her, not while they were in uniform. She'd never hated that reg so much as she did right now. "Mac, I'll fill you in on the rest later. But thanks for letting me know about the climate out there. I think we need to call a formation for 1100 and lay out all the facts we can."

"I'll put the word out." Mac glanced at her, questioning without words whether it was really okay to leave.

She nodded once, and he stepped out, making apologies as he closed the door.

At the click of the latch, Cassidy leaned against the side of her desk and eyed Shane. He'd just had a shower. She could smell his shampoo from here. The scent lit nerve endings she'd forgotten she had. He wore his uniform, beret tucked into the leg pocket, cloth hugging his shoulders, and the cut emphasizing his slim hips. What she wouldn't give to grab him by the arm and force him to run away with her right now...forever.

Except she'd never been one to run away. "You made me weak."

"Come again?" Shane's eyebrows drew together into a dark V. "I did what?"

"You made me cry. Now I just want to...give up." Cassidy crossed her arms and dropped her gaze to the floor in front of his feet, wishing for normal, for a way to make the chaos go away and to still have him here with her.

In two steps he was to her, his hands gripping her shoulders. "Cassy, you can't give up. You haven't done anything wrong." His fingers tightened as though he wanted to defy regs and pull her closer. "You and I both know you're innocent of anything they say, whether it's murder or smuggling or something else we haven't even dreamed yet."

"What if you're wrong?" She shook her head and squeezed her eyes tight, hating herself for her thoughts and for her weakness.

"I can't be. But..." He released her and stepped back. "I didn't make it to your house in time."

Her jaw went slack with the whiplash of the conversation, but his words dug in and raised the practical part of her. "They beat you there?"

"They had a warrant. Your landlord let them in."

Cassidy sank onto the edge of the desk and gripped it until her knuckles went white. "So now I have no idea what they've got on me."

"That was your only copy?"

She fidgeted with the pocket on the sleeve of her uniform. "Stupidly... Yes." She closed her eyes and hoped to open them to find out this was the most drawn-out nightmare in history. With a deep breath, she peeked at the room. No such luck. "Now what? I'm fresh out of ideas."

"I wanted to get a look at your soldiers again, and I figured it'd be best to blend in. Somebody here knows something, and watching might tell me what it is."

"You didn't ask me if it was okay."

"You're going to tell me you *don't* suspect them?"

Once again, Shane called her out. He'd read her mind since the day she met him. She should have remembered that little ability of his sooner. She just hoped he couldn't read her emotions, too, because all she wanted to do right now was sink into his arms and let him handle everything. Holding herself up was getting to be too hard and she knew, somehow, Shane would find a way to chase all of the bad things away. Except… She'd always prided herself on being strong, and no matter what had changed between the two of them, she couldn't start playing the damsel in distress now. "No. You can't stay."

The denial filtered into Shane's understanding. "No? Cassy, I—"

"You'll hurt more than help. You're walking into a climate where these soldiers have just lost a buddy, and they suspect it was because somebody took him out. CID has crawled all over my office and won't let them into their own building. And you think you can walk in here in your uniform and start asking questions? You didn't think this through, and you'll wind up with nothing but a bunch of soldiers who all act weird at the sight of you, because this whole day is out of control."

"What are you going to do?"

It took a few cycles for her brain to catch up to the question. She'd been prepared for an argument, not a complete conversational shift. "I've called formation before lunch, then I guess I'll go home." *If I'm not in jail.*

Shane stood and drew his beret between his fingers, his green eyes searching her face. "I'm leaving this building right now, but I'm not going anywhere. Do you understand that?"

Her fingertips tingled, and she couldn't swallow. It took a moment for her to find her voice. "I understand."

With a nod, Shane hesitated, then gripped his beret tighter and disappeared out the door.

With the rigger shed closed for business and the bulk of the warehouselike building cordoned off by yellow crime scene tape, Cassidy had cut loose her riggers after the 1100 briefing where Mac laid out everything the authorities would let them tell. It hadn't done much to defuse the dynamite sizzling in the air around the shed, but maybe an afternoon off would temper feelings.

Her office was eerie and silent. It made the back of her neck tingle, and those invisible eyes stood menacing vigil over her again.

With Shane gone, the building grew emptier still. The fact made her angry with herself. It was one thing to realize she still loved him, but quite another to surrender to weakness. No matter what, she had to stay strong, even if it meant holding Shane at arm's length for a little while longer.

But now, her strength was failing.

Last night she'd thought about telling the authorities—namely Special Agent Watters—everything that had happened. Aware such a late admission at the wrong time could swing the eyes of suspicion her way, she'd felt it better for the moment to remain silent. They'd find out Shane had called the police to her house soon enough. With her computers confiscated and her house searched, it now seemed her silence had only served to boost her to the status of prime suspect.

Cassidy tapped her fingers on the desk and studied her reflection in the windows across the room. It seemed to be a pretty accurate picture of her life up until this morning. A woman, alone, in the middle of a big empty space with no anchor. Another glance at the windows reminded her exactly what her show of strength had netted. A life alone, her only friend someone who had been paid to spy on her. Even Shane, though he'd admitted he still loved her, had said he couldn't be her "savior."

Savior. Her fingers stilled on the desktop. What was it he'd said? She struggled to remember the words. *That's God's job...and I've overstepped His bounds.*

The statement mixed with the chaplain's words the night before and jelled into concrete thought. Shane couldn't save her. As hard as he'd tried, she still found herself mired deeper with each revelation. It was clearer with every breath she couldn't save herself either. She'd turned everywhere...except to God.

Other than her silent prayers at Jackson's apartment and in the rigger shed last night, it had been years since God had even been a consideration. Faith had been the core part of her until her father was diagnosed with cancer. She'd prayed God would save him... Prayed He'd bring her fellow soldiers safely home... Prayed He'd save her marriage... And He hadn't. He hadn't done any of those things. With each negative answer, her faith ebbed until it disappeared over the horizon.

But the last one was her fault. In her blind anger and immaturity, she'd shoved Shane out of her life. Now he was back, just when she needed him most, the answer to a prayer she hadn't even dared to speak but knew now she'd been praying all along. She'd never truly given up on Shane. What she'd given up on was God. And Shane was right. No one else could save her.

Without another second's hesitation, she rested her head on the desk. For several ticks of the clock, no words formed. What could she say to Someone she'd ignored and railed against for so many years? The chaplain's words—the same ones that had led her to apologize to Shane in the early hours of this morning—rushed back. "I'm sorry."

Other than fresh tears on the edges of her eyelashes, nothing happened. She didn't know what she expected but felt compelled to keep going. "I'm sorry for trying to do this on my own. I can't. And I feel like a hypocrite coming to You now, but all I've managed to do is make a huge mess. And whether You fix that or not, I can't carry myself anymore. I need Your help."

Cassidy drew in a deep breath and lifted her head, surprised to feel like her lungs filled completely. For the first time in memory, it didn't feel like the weight of her entire life bent her double. He'd taken it. *Thank you.* The words wouldn't greet the air, but she knew her heart was heard.

Right now, she wanted nothing more than to tell Shane, and then she had a lot to spill to the authorities. Cassidy reached for her cell phone but stopped, her fingers twitching. No, she'd tell him in person.

As she stood, she stooped to grab her laptop bag and froze. Her personal laptop. It had been on her the whole time. The one computer the investigators hadn't taken with them. It hadn't been in the house during either invasion. The first time it had been with…

Jackson. Her fingers worried the strap of her bag. As a federal agent, he couldn't be behind all of this. It had to be coincidence that he'd been with her when her house was invaded. And he'd found her "lost" ID card, the very ID card needed to access her work computer. There was something else, something that tugged at the corner of a memory but she couldn't quite pull it into the light. Something about Jackson.

If only there was a way to find out how much truth he told.

A single thought dragged in relief with a splash of condemnation. There was one way to find a hint, and she should have thought of it long before now. Cassidy slid her laptop bag onto the desk, then slipped across the room to check the outer office and peer down at the floor below. The building was empty. She could search her computer without fear of someone telling the authorities they'd missed one.

The machine loaded slower than ever, and Cassidy tapped her fingers against the keyboard while she waited. Her eyes stayed locked on her phone. Should she call Shane now, before she knew anything, or wait to see if her suspicions had legs?

A phone call from Shane. That was it. The niggling memory burst into full sunlight. Shane had called to warn her Jackson was in on it, but she'd never asked why he thought so. He'd seen something, something that convinced him the other man was trouble.

Cassidy snatched the cell, pressed the last number dialed, and held the phone between her shoulder and her ear as she brought up the Freemail website. She dug through her planner, found the small piece of paper and keyed in the email address and password she'd seen tacked to Jackson's computer monitor. Adrenaline winged thoughts through her head. What if she was wrong? Or worse, what if she was right?

"Cassy? Everything okay?" Shane's voice brought her typing to a stuttered stop.

"Yeah, listen. Really quick because I'm thinking something," Cassidy flexed her fingers and admonished her heart. Now was not the time to get into emotional revelations. "Where are you?"

"Your house. I wanted to see if they found your hard drive. Why?"

"When you called me yesterday, what made you think Jackson was involved?"

The silence grew brittle, then Shane muttered something so low it was barely audible, although it sounded like the word *stupid* was involved. "Cassy, get back to your house. Now."

Cassidy gripped the phone and lifted her head. "Shane?"

"I blew it." More muttering tickled her ear before he said, "You never saw a badge or any kind of ID at all, did you?"

"No." She dropped her head onto her hand. "And papers like the ones he showed me are way too easy to forge."

"Jackson has to be part of it. I saw him yesterday with the man who blew up Anderson's car."

"That information would have been good to have last night." Cassidy clicked on the sent email box and scanned the results, then bit back a word she typically didn't even dare to think. Bile burned a path from her stomach to her throat, and she swallowed twice, her muscles weakening with fear and anger.

"He set me up." Her voice squeaked like a misblown clarinet, and her eyes drifted shut.

"What?"

"On his desk he had an email address and a password and it's… There are dozens of emails here, all with my signature, all coordinating the whole thing. Shipment dates, contacts, dollar amounts, everything. He had my laptop all weekend, plenty of time to do whatever he wanted." Derek's words as he rifled through the files on her computer crashed reality into the fog. Her throat closed and she forced the thought into the air. "That interface card Derek found. That's why they needed access to my computers."

Shane's exhale burst against her eardrum. "They sent the emails from one computer, then switched cards to make it look like they came from your computer."

"And I've got no proof."

"I'd say you have too much proof." A rustle at the door jerked Cassidy's head up to find the owner of the female voice.

Sergeant Erin Landon stood in the doorway, but Cassidy's eyes saw only the gun in her hand. "What—"

"Hang up the phone, Chief. We need to have a little chat."

SIXTEEN

"Cassy!" Shane shouted into the phone, knowing all the while there was no ear on the other end to hear. A startled exclamation, a second voice and she was gone. Fingers frantic, he redialed her number, but the phone passed to voice mail.

If anything happened to her, he'd spend the rest of his life punishing Jackson Reese—or whatever his name really was—and himself for being so unbelievably stupid. His shock at Cassidy's revelation that Jackson was an agent had overridden everything else, driving him to doubt what his own eyes had seen. He should have told her yesterday, should have insisted she double check, should have asked if she saw a badge instead of assuming she had. Instead, he'd let relief at her momentary safety override his common sense.

Now all he had was a useless rush of adrenaline. To rush to the rigger shed now like a misguided knight in shining armor wouldn't get him a thing. By the time he got there, Cassy would be long gone or…so much worse. And having her cell phone's position triangulated by the authorities would likely lead them straight to her office. There was no way whoever had her would be stupid enough to bring that phone along with them.

Fear like none he'd ever known ate at the edges of his reasoning. Focus. He had to focus. He tightened his grip on his own phone and hesitated before his fingers pushed 9-1-1 on the screen.

The moment the operator answered, the word spilled out. "This is Major Shane Logan. I need to either be patched through to post or you need to contact emergency services now to get the MPs to the rigger shed."

"Sir, what's your emergency?" The operator's calm voice in the face of Cassy's danger nearly blew the last of his patience through the ceiling.

"At the rigger shed, right now. Someone is kidnapping my wife." The instant the word hit his ears, his voice died. His *wife*. The word gripped him along with the panic. Had he ever really thought of her as anything else?

"Sir, what makes you say that?"

As quickly as he could spew the words, Shane laid out an outline of the last few days, wishing the guy on the other end of the line would just get it and move on. This wasn't the time for stories. Cassy needed help.

Precious minutes ticked by as Shane paced the

kitchen floor and waited for confirmation. He'd been trained to be a man of action, not to be a man of passivity and, right now, this was the most helpless he'd ever been. For the first time in his life, there was nothing he could do. Nothing.

Except pray.

The words tumbled in his head in a jumble of sounds with no cohesion. But God knew. He had to know. He'd hit the wall, the place where it was going to have to be the Spirit and not him, because there were no words.

"Sir?" The operator's voice drew Shane's thoughts to a halt. "I patched through to Fort Bragg. The Military Police are on their way. Where are you now?"

Keys. Where were his truck keys? There was no way he was going to stand here and wait if he could do one single thing to help. "I'm on my way there." Before the operator could protest, he killed the call and shoved the phone into his hip pocket. He found his keys on the kitchen counter and bolted for the door leading to the garage as his mind whirled. It had been a female voice drifting across her phone.

Shane yanked the door open. And if a female was with Cassy, then either Jackson was telling the truth or he was—

"You don't know how long I've waited to do this." Jackson stood at the top of the steps.

Reflex balled Shane's fingers into a fist, but surprise provided his enemy with the advantage. A brief flash of Jackson's smirk, a blow to the jaw... and darkness.

Shane's truck sat in the driveway to the left of the garage. Relief flooded Cassidy, dulling the burn where plastic zip-tie handcuffs chafed and dug at her wrists. Erin Landon couldn't go much further with this, not if Shane had anything to say about it.

Tapping the garage door remote in the Trailblazer, Erin shot Cassidy a sideway glance. "I wouldn't breathe too easily, Chief. If my timing's right, you've got a man in that house who's just a few minutes from putting a gun to his own head."

"Shane would never—"

"Maybe not." Erin shifted the truck into Park and closed the garage door, then pocketed the opener and left the truck's engine running. Her eyes searched Cassidy's face for a reaction. "But it sure is going to look like he did."

"You can't kill more people and expect the authorities to be stupid." Cassidy wriggled her wrists and fought to kick above panic into breathable air at the surface. Going out in her own house was never part of the plan. *God, I can't do this on my own.* Surely God wouldn't accept her surrender and then take her off the planet just a couple of hours later.

"Oh, you mean Anderson? Poor guy. It would have been a nice, tidy suicide if Jackson had used his head and made the rope long enough for the private to reach those controls. He's a charming guy, but not the smartest one I ever partnered with." She shrugged and leveled her gaze out the windshield, one foot on the ground and one still in the car. "See? Now, that one's all your ex-husband, jealous as he was to see you talking to another man, he just couldn't take it. It doesn't take much money to buy a few eyewitnesses who'll say they saw him lurking around the shed that night."

Erin had thought everything through. Surely there was a hole somewhere, a hole big enough to let Cassidy crawl through and escape. If she could just keep the younger woman talking long enough, the solution was bound to come. "Your money couldn't buy Anderson's silence, could it?"

"Nope, and neither could torching his car. He was planning to go to you with the fact we paid him off for his help, so Jackson thought he needed a little nudge to keep quiet. It worked out well, though. That distraction gave us the perfect opportunity to switch out your ID card and your office keys with fakes, but none of us could crack your password and access your computer. You changed it Friday, didn't you?"

Cassidy smirked. God was looking out for her even before she asked Him to.

"Make faces all you want, Chief. I've still got the gun. Now slide over here into the driver's seat and do it slowly. If you give me any reason to worry, one warning shot from me will prompt a not-so-warning shot from Jackson."

Plans flipped through Cassidy's mind and were discarded as quickly as they appeared. This idea too risky... That idea too slow... More time. If only she had more time. "Why? Why put money in the hands of the people shooting at you?"

"Really?" Landon's fingers tightened on the pistol's grip. "We funnel billions into that country, then we go fight their war on a soldier's salary. What's wrong with playing middleman for them and getting a little bit back?"

Cassidy fought not to let her revulsion show. Her own sense of duty couldn't begin to comprehend something so mercenary. She eyed the driver's seat, then flicked her eyes to Erin. From this awkward angle, there was no way to launch her body across the console with enough force to take the other woman down. Trapped, with no way to tell whether Shane was dead or alive, she couldn't tell if Erin Landon told the truth or painted a vibrant lie.

"Take all the time you need. Pretty soon you'll figure out there's nowhere to go."

With a deep sigh, Cassidy eased herself across the truck, wincing at the bite of plastic into flesh. She might be at a disadvantage, but she wasn't done yet. "Shane has an alibi for the night Anderson died."

Confusion flickered across Erin's features before they molded into marble so cold that it shuddered

Cassidy's stomach. She yanked a zip tie from the leg pocket of her ACU, slid the gun into her hip pocket, jerked Cassidy's arms up to the steering wheel and locked the plastic cuffs to the vinyl before retrieving the gun. "No matter. There's one more person who can be blamed for that. In fact," she tapped her finger against the barrel of the gun and smiled, "it might work out better for me anyway."

Light and sound returned to Shane's world at a slow cadence that marched to the throb of his pulse. Electric pain jolted through his jaw, past his teeth and into the back of his neck. Nausea rode waves through his body. His head thumped with every beat of his heart. Man, this one would hurt for a long time to come.

His eyes jerked behind closed eyelids with the returning memory of Jackson's sneer. Then again, it would probably only hurt for the rest of his life. By his current calculations, that might not be a very respectable period of time.

Groaning, he eased his neck around and felt the burn into his spine, then edged his eyes open.

"I think slow works just fine. It might even keep you alive a few minutes longer."

Shane blinked Jackson into focus. Where… Without moving his head, he let his eyes roam. Cassidy's living room. Shane lay prone between the coffee table and the TV, Jackson's leather-clad foot short inches from his nose. "Where's Cassy?"

"Well, I heard the garage door open a few minutes ago. My guess is she's teetering on the edge of a nice, peaceful death once the carbon monoxide gets to work."

Relief and fear waged a firefight in Shane's chest. Cassy was still alive, but not for long unless he screwed his head back on straight and took Jackson down. He sneaked another peek. Unless he took Jackson and his gun down. First a blade and now a bullet. If he wanted to come out of this alive, it would take a whole lot more than him to do it.

More than him. Shane's eyes slipped shut again. *You're probably the only one who can get us out of this, God. Just give me something to work with here.* "You don't have it in you to kill Cassy." He'd seen the look in Jackson's eye at the rigger shed. No, the man wasn't in love with her, but he felt something more than predator and prey.

"You're right, I can't. I'm not that great at killing, just not built that way. Had the chance and didn't take it. After a year with her, I got a taste of why you married her. If she'd lived, some guy out there eventually would have been lucky. I tried to break her down a few times, see if I couldn't mix a little pleasure with business, but it never worked."

Shane's muscles clenched so tight that his eyes

widened and watered with the pain. What he wouldn't give to shove his fist right through—

"Nope, never worked. She's still in love with you." He passed the gun to his left hand and flexed the fingers of his right, glancing at Shane's jaw. "Just one of the dozen reasons that felt so good."

As much as Shane wanted to launch himself into a brawl, the fight would be one-sided as long as bullets were involved. Instead he waited. He rolled onto his side and took his time testing muscles. When distraction came, he'd be ready to move. And the distraction would come. It had to. He'd asked for it, and he couldn't force himself to believe everything ended here.

"I can't kill her, but the world's going to think you did."

Shane's muscles locked. "I'd never—"

"You couldn't take it when she rejected you, and you couldn't bear to watch her die. You and I are alike that way, huh? So you used the exhaust from her own car to poison her. And then," Jackson aimed the gun at Shane, "you killed yourself." A sharp kick to Shane's wounded shoulder forced him onto his back, new pain burning a path through his arm. "You should have stayed out of it, Major. Then Cassidy would be alive. In jail for setting up a drug ring, but alive."

Playing hurt would keep him alive a lot longer than a show of strength, and it would keep Jackson talking in the arrogance of his perceived authority. Shane gripped his arm and groaned, hoping it would sound believable. "So you're the ringleader of this whole thing?"

Jackson shook his head. "Nah, I'm just the pretty face. Erin's got a mind for this stuff, but the Taliban would never respect a woman. Everything's set up with her name and my face. Works well, huh?"

A woman. It could be anybody. *Keep him talking. Just a little while longer.* "But why Cassy?"

"Because she was the one in charge when we got everything set up to roll. Wasn't hard to get a contractor job in her radius. She's a tough one to get to trust you, though. That took some time. I almost hate they intercepted our very first shipment out, and we had to set her up so fast. I wouldn't have minded hanging around for a while longer."

Shane gritted his teeth. Jackson was goading him, poking fingers into raw wounds to get a reaction. In about ten seconds, Shane would give him a reaction, right in his windpipe.

Footsteps in the kitchen broke his focus and drew his eye. The faint scent of exhaust fumes followed the sound. He was running short on time.

When the uniformed soldier stepped into the living room, instant relief melted Shane's readiness... Until he saw the gun she carried with casual familiarity. He knew this woman, a rigger in Cassy's company, the same one who'd set off alarms in her office.

The sergeant never even glanced at Shane. Her focus lay on Jackson. "So, there's a little problem with the major here."

Jackson made the ultimate stupid move and turned his back on Shane, but it did little good. Shane needed to pull down two people at once, and they stood too far apart for him to hit them both.

"What's the problem?"

"He's got an alibi for last night. We can't put it on either one of them."

Cursing, Jackson spun to look down at Shane. "Now what?" Before Shane could cover, a sharp boot to the side spun a crack and blue agony across his vision. He strained to breathe, but his lungs wouldn't take it. He wasn't faking weakness this time. The low whimper that escaped as he drew himself to his hands and knees was real.

Not now. Not a broken rib now.

"Have you lost your mind? They're supposed to believe he killed her and then himself. The more you pound on him, the less they're going to buy that. I'm already going to plan B. I don't have time to come up with plan C."

"When did we come up with a plan B?" Jackson breathed hard as he glared down at Shane. The man may say he wasn't big on killing, but the look in his eye said Shane might be the one to destroy that conviction.

The sergeant raised her weapon. "About two minutes ago." Without hesitating, she twitched her finger and fired.

No. Cassidy wrenched to the side as the gunshot cracked over the hum of the engine. Her forehead sank to her bound wrists, and tears stung her wounds. She drew a deep breath and coughed on exhaust fumes, a dull headache working its way into her forehead.

On a surge of anger, she jerked her wrists over and over again, tearing skin. "No. No. No. No!" Swallowing hard, she refused to give in to tears. As long as she was breathing, she could fight. Even if Shane was...

"No." It was the only word she had to beat back the image of Shane and blood and pain. She'd been stupid so many years ago, stupid five days ago and stupid today when she didn't open that phone call with the news that God had finally grabbed her. She finally understood. Shane didn't want to be needed, he needed to be wanted. God should be the only one she needed. But oh, she wanted Shane.

She twisted her wrists until the painful cut of plastic danced spots before her eyes. It was too late, and it was useless. Without a knife she'd never be able to cut through the zip ties. She ground her teeth together. There were two knives within arm's length, one in the console and one in the glove box. Fat lot of good they did her now.

Overcome with frustration and gnawing fear, Cassidy stomped her foot. The engine revved, and she yanked her leg back. She was still alive until everything went dark, and gunning the engine would only kill her faster.

Gunning the engine...

Cassidy's entire body tingled as she eased down on the accelerator and let up, then rested her gaze on the automatic gearshift on the steering column. Maybe... Maybe there was a way out after all, but she'd only get one shot.

Grimacing against the pain as the cuffs dug deeper, she pulled her left leg up and crossed it over her right thigh, heel against the button on the shifter. One notch. All she needed to do was click it back one notch. Any more would drive the car forward into the wall.

She eased the shifter into Reverse with her booted heel, dropped her foot to the brake, then slid her right foot to the gas. With another prayer on her lips, she pressed the accelerator to the floor.

Tires screamed... Rubber burned... And Cassidy snapped her foot off the brake.

"What—"

Now. Now might be the only chance he got. As

the sergeant turned at the shriek of tires and the crash in the garage, Shane gathered everything he had left in reserve and sprung, aiming his good shoulder at the center of her back.

The impact jarred the air from his lungs, and the gun bounced off the door frame and into the kitchen. The pair landed with a dull thud that rocked Shane's fragile grip on consciousness. Gasping for air, he wrapped his arm around her neck, forced her chin up with his elbow and squeezed to cut off blood flow until the sergeant went limp beneath him. After an extra second to be sure she was unconscious, he let her go and rolled onto his side, cradling his aching ribs and trying in vain to take a deep breath.

Cassy. She was still alive.

And with blood flowing freely again, there was a short window during which the sergeant would stay down. Easing to his feet, Shane glanced around the room for anything that would restrain her. He ripped the table lamp from the wall and used the cord to truss her hands as tightly as he could with his side screaming. It wouldn't stop her, but it might slow her down.

Jackson struggled to sit up, right hand gripping his left shoulder as blood seeped between his fingers. "Did she really—"

"'Fraid so, man." Shane kicked Jackson's gun out of reach and knelt beside him as he propped against the couch. "Good thing she's a bad shot. She aimed too high for your heart."

"Lucky me." Pain and shock ebbed the fight out of Jackson as Shane pressed a throw pillow against his shoulder and pushed Jackson's hand against it.

Shane heaved himself up and hesitated, torn at the thought of never leaving anybody behind, but time wasn't on his side. "Hold that. At least we know you won't bleed to death before somebody gets here." He didn't wait for a response, but retrieved the gun and stumbled into the kitchen. Pocketing the second gun, he burst through the door, fighting the pain in his ribs for air.

Cassidy's Trailblazer rested half in and half out of the garage, the metal door crumpled around it. When she saw him, her eyes widened, then tears chased shock down her face. They were alive. Both of them were alive.

Shane's stagger to the driver's side door seemed to take hours, but he finally made it and yanked the truck open. "Need some help?" He shoved the car into Park and killed the engine.

"They didn't shoot you?" Cassidy's words tight-roped on thick emotion. He was alive. A bruise formed along his jaw and he favored his side, but he was alive.

"Shoot me? Nah." From the sounds of it, a crowd gathered in the driveway on the other side of the garage door. Sirens rose and fell in increasing proximity. "Want me to get you out of here before the police bust in?" His gaze fell to her wrists and his eyes flashed lightning. He flinched. "I ought to go back in there and…"

She couldn't pull her eyes from his face. He was alive, and she loved him. And he needed to know what she hadn't said last night. "Just… There's a knife in the console. Cut me out of here. Please."

When Shane leaned across her, she caught her breath and wished more than ever to be free to wrap her arms around him. He backed away before she was ready.

"Who called the police?" His focus remained on his work as he tried to slice through her bonds without digging them farther into her flesh.

Cassidy tilted her head to the console above the rearview mirror and focused on anything other than the pain. "My car. Crash response. I thought about trying to stretch my foot up there to hit the call button, but it was easier to take out the garage door and let it call for itself."

With a snap, her hands pulled free and she exhaled the breath she'd held since her eyes first rested on that gun. Now. Now she could tell him.

Shane grabbed her elbow and yanked her from the car. No once-over of her wrists, no "happy to see you alive," no nothing, just a rough tug.

Cassidy resisted. "Shane."

The tone of her voice drew hesitation.

She swallowed the fear that he'd reject her once again. "I'm still in love with you, too."

For the briefest instant, his eyes held hers and softened into sea green, then he gripped her elbow tighter. "Get out the side door. Go."

"I—"

Dull eyes searched her face, then he shoved her toward the door. "Just go."

SEVENTEEN

"For the last time, I said no." Shane shrugged off the paramedic, trying not to scream in pain as he did. The face of the woman who attempted to take his vital signs barely registered. All of his attention was across the front yard on Cassy. She sat on the front porch with Derek, wrapped in a blanket and surrounded by police officers and more paramedics.

The police had sorted out the stories and determined that Erin and Jackson were the bad guys... although Shane held all of the weapons. Jackson had been loaded into the first ambulance on the scene and carted to the hospital, spilling everything to anyone who would listen. Erin hadn't been far behind, hands properly restrained in handcuffs instead of electrical cord.

Shane gave his side of the story to the police and now fought off the paramedics and EMTs who wanted to take him to the hospital for X-rays and "real" stitches.

"Sir, you need to let us transport you."

Shane tore his eyes from Cassy to the man who obviously outranked all of the other firemen and medical personnel on scene. "I respect you're trying to do your job, but it's a broken rib. They won't even tape it if I go in. Just give me that little refusal of transport thing and let me stay here. I need to…" He needed to what? Talk to Cassy? Explain he'd kicked her out of the house after she'd said she loved him because he was terrified she was still in danger? None of that would fly with the man who stood in front of him, he was sure.

"I'll tell you what." Shane swiveled his gaze to the older man, whose expression said he knew exactly where Shane's head was. "You promise me you'll have that young lady take you in for a look-over, and I'll give you the form to sign." He stuck out a thick hand. "Deal?"

Shane bit the inside of his lower lip to capture a smile. "Deal, sir." He signed his name with a flourish, eased off the back of the ambulance and made the slow walk across the lawn to Cassy.

When Derek saw him coming, he said something to Cassy and corralled the remaining paramedics in the vicinity, then headed for the small cluster of emergency vehicles that sat in the driveway. As he passed Shane, he tipped his head. "Don't blow it this time, dude."

Shane ignored the jab and dipped a grateful nod at his friend, then turned his attention to Cassy. She looked helpless with the white cotton blanket slipping off one shoulder and her wrists swathed in pure bandages. The sight of them blew the heat of rage through him anew. The idea that they'd hurt her...

It took a deep breath to stem the rage as he nodded to the step beside her. "May I?"

She shrugged and dropped her gaze to the ground. The adrenaline was draining out of her, and she'd grown as pale and gray as the cement on which she sat.

He settled beside her, his good arm brushing her elbow. "You smell like the pits at a NASCAR race."

"You sure do know how to sweet-talk a woman, Logan."

"What did the paramedics say?"

"They said I should thank God for the catalytic converter on the truck. Carbon monoxide would have killed me eventually if I'd been in there long enough, but because of the emissions standards now there wasn't as much coming in. Worst I'll have to deal with is this vicious headache."

Shane beat back residual fear as it tried to blow through his body like an explosive. He'd almost lost her for good. "So, Erin's bullet apparently unhinged Jackson's mouth."

"Yeah?" Cassy's mouth pulled into a slight frown. "Hope he's saying enough to prove I'm innocent."

The betrayal was still fresh for her. It was written in the lines around her mouth. Shane would do anything to erase that look. "He is. I think he decided he's already in enough trouble, and when she shot him, all bets were off. Seems the plan all along was to set up whoever sat in your chair. They just didn't count on getting busted their first shipment out. They tried to set you up and everything fell apart."

"Their setup wasn't in place." Cassy's fingers found a loose string on the edge of the blanket. It stole her focus as she worked it around her knuckle. "They thought they had more time to get to my computers."

"Or to convince you Jackson was on your side. That got moved up, too." Shane reached for her hand and rested his fingers over hers, stilling the restless picking. "That whole thing at his apartment... He had two options."

"Kill me or make me trust him until they had what they needed." She sniffed, her fingers tightening beneath his. "They didn't give Anderson that option, did they?"

"I got the impression from all of the babbling that murder was never option one, but Erin's pretty cold-blooded. She saw a way to throw even more suspicion your way." He cleared his throat and tried to catch her eye, but she stared at their hands. This next part might not be any easier for her to hear. "They... The police found the guy who blew up Anderson's car."

"Yeah?"

"Erin was cleaning house after her shipment was diverted. She panicked. She took out Anderson and then took down the guy who was doing her dirty work. He's the one who broke into your house. Jackson's lucky she's got terrible aim."

"And we were next." Her voice rasped low.

That was it. He couldn't take it anymore. As gently as he could against the pain waving through him, he wrapped an arm around her shoulder and pulled her close. "Cassy, I—"

She didn't hesitate but leaned into him in a way she hadn't for years. "I know. You shoved me out the door because you knew it wasn't over yet, not with Jackson and Erin still in the house."

"Yeah."

"I heard her shoot Jackson, and I thought you were…" The words melted into gibberish as sobs shook her.

Shane tightened his grip and pulled her against his shoulder, her tears soaking through his shirt and baptizing him with the love she'd confessed such a short time ago. He let her cry, relished her in his arms, not willing to ever push her away again. His own eyes grew wet and he blinked twice. As much as he wanted to put this all behind them and move forward to normal, to address her words in the garage, he wasn't sure now was the time for Cassy, not with her emotions in turmoil and her life more chaotic than any spy novel.

In spite of everything they'd been through and said, some small part of him still expected her to turn her back and walk away again. If she did that, it would rip holes in places he'd never be able to repair. That was a fear that had to die. He just wasn't sure how to kill it.

"And that's when I knew you were right." Cassy sniffed and pulled away from him, swiping her eyes with the edges of the blanket.

He'd missed something. "Say that again?" His heart picked up speed. Somehow, he knew what she'd just said, even though his ears hadn't understood a word of it.

"You said I wanted you to save me, and I wasn't trusting God to do it. You were right. I quit trusting God long before my father died... Until this afternoon, in my office, before I called you."

This was no battlefield conversion she was talking about. Emotion lodged in his throat and roughened the edges of his voice. "You're saying..."

"That I figured it out. Sometimes God says no to our prayers. And sometimes He says yes." She lifted her face to meet his eyes. "Either way, He knows more than we do, better than we do. We have to trust Him. We have to trust His timing." Her expression spoke the rest of the thought without the need for words.

God's timing. For them. It was no coincidence Shane was the one to come across the intel that led him to Cassy's parking lot. It was no coincidence that put him there the moment Anderson's car blew. It was no coincidence whatsoever that their lives had intersected at the exact moment when she'd needed God—and Shane—the most.

But still, he needed confirmation, needed to hear her speak out loud the words she was hinting. "So what are you saying exactly?"

She searched his face for long breaths before she spoke, tightening his chest and driving uncertainty deeper into his heart. What if he was wrong? "I did that to you." Her index finger rested against the outside corner of his eye. "I put that fear there."

If he denied it, it would be the biggest lie he'd ever told.

"You were always fearless, while I was the one wrapped up in what might happen, all of the ways I could lose you. I needed you too much, put too much on you, asked you to be something you could never be. I think it was easier to push you away than to risk your vanishing in a way that was out of my control."

Her hand dropped to her lap and sought his. She gripped his fingers so tightly in hers that he fought the urge to wince. The lights of the emergency vehicles, the murmur of voices, the urgency of the past few days all faded as his focus drew tight on the narrow space around them. "Don't do that to me again." His voice was too husky, too hoarse, giving away everything he wanted to cover until she spoke the words.

"I won't." The way her eyes held his without flinching spoke more than the words she was saying. "You can't be my everything. It's not humanly possible." She swallowed so hard that Shane could see it, her eyes dipping and coming back to his, more certain than ever. "But I want you to be everything you're supposed to be. To me."

Shane's heart beat so hard his ribs throbbed, but he didn't care. Right here, in the small space around them on her front porch, was a moment he never thought he'd live to see, a moment for which he'd ached a decade, a moment that swept away all fear.

"You're sure?"

A smile quirked the corner of her lips. "As sure as I am that you and I are both here and still breathing after everything that's happened." Any amusement she'd been working up faded. "It took me too long to figure it out, but I do still love you."

With a trembling hand, Shane reached up and brushed dark blond hair from green-gold eyes. It was his privilege, and he'd do everything in his power never to lose it again. His fingers slid down her cheek to her chin, where one finger hooked and lifted her face to his. Just before his lips brushed hers, he whispered, "And I love you."

EPILOGUE

"Therefore, if anyone is in Christ, he is a new creation; the old has gone, the new has come." Chaplain Ferguson spoke the words of II Corinthians 5:17 as though he knew what they meant to Cassidy's heart.

She wrinkled her nose to keep back a giggle. After all of the premarital counseling he'd insisted Shane and she do before he'd agreed to perform this ceremony, he probably grasped exactly how those words spoke to her.

Shane leaned down toward her, and the sleeve of his dress blues brushed her arm. His breath tickled her ear and sent warm shivers across her neck. "It's not polite to smirk during your own benediction, Mrs. Logan. What will our parents think?"

This time, the smile wouldn't stay hidden. "That's Chief Logan to you, Major," she whispered, then tipped her head to meet those amazing green eyes. "And our parents will think," she nearly choked on the emotion, "that we're happy."

Chaplain Ferguson's voice cut through their whispers. "You may now kiss the bride."

Shane pulled her to him. "And we are." His lips moved against hers almost silently. "Very happy."

Cassidy gave her all to the kiss that cemented her to Shane—and to God's will—for the rest of her life.

* * * * *

Dear Reader,

Thank you so much for joining me on this journey to Fort Bragg, North Carolina. I'd be honored if you'd also stand with me in saluting the brave men and women who rotate through the post in the continual fight for our freedom. Some of the greatest soldiers I know have been stationed there, including my husband of sixteen years. I'm partial to the place. It's where I met him.

Cassidy and Shane's journey was a long one for me. Smack in the middle of the first draft, my husband left for his third deployment. If you are a military spouse, you know how it is. A part of you disappears right along with them, packed in an olive drab duffel bag next to their combat boots and Kevlar. It was a real adventure learning how to write with the better half of me slogging through combat half a world away, but God handled it and grew both of us in ways we never imagined.

This story challenged me in another way. When I started, Cassidy's independent streak had not yet revealed itself. The more she came to life on the page, the more I realized her battle was my own. Self-reliance is an amazing thing, especially when someone you love is in the military. But too much self-reliance can come back to beat you into the ground. We weren't meant to handle everything on our own. That's why God didn't wind up the watch of this world and take His hand away. He's right here, every second, caring about every breath we take. Too often, we present only the big stuff to Him, figuring we can handle the small stuff on our own. As both Cassidy and Shane learned, our own strength will carry us only so far. God created us to need Him, so isn't it high time we started leaning on Him a little harder?

I hope you've enjoyed *Freefall*. I'd love it if you dropped by to say hi to me. You can find me on the web at www.jodiebailey.com and as a contributor to the military family blog www.winningthewarat home.blogspot.com, or you can drop an email to Jodie@jodiebailey.com. Thank you so much for reading. You touch my heart more than you will ever know!

Jodie Bailey

Questions for Discussion

1. Have you ever lost a friend or a loved one because of a misunderstanding? Was it resolved? If not, what would it take to reach a resolution and to make amends?

2. Cassidy lost nearly everyone she cared about in a short period of time: several fellow soldiers, her husband and her father. Has there ever been a season in your life when it seemed everything was taken away from you? How did you cope? What did that do to your faith?

3. The main theme of the novel is trust: trust in other people, trust in ourselves and trust in God. We all go through seasons where our ability to trust is tested. How do you face those seasons?

4. When your faith is tested, where do you go to find strength?

5. Cassidy is betrayed by Jackson, someone she considers to be a close friend. Have you ever been betrayed by someone you cared about? What happened to that relationship? Were you able to forgive?

6. One of the weaknesses in Cassidy and Shane's marriage was the amount of time they were apart. What are some ways you can keep distant loved ones close? Is it possible to nurture a relationship over a distance? If you are a military spouse, how have you stayed close to your loved one over extended training exercises and deployments?

7. What has been your biggest crisis of faith? Are you still in it? How did you resolve it?

8. Derek is the kind of friend who "tells it like it is." How important is it to have someone like that in your life? Do you respect or resent someone who confronts you with the truth?

9. Shane realizes his arrogance has led him to try to solve all of Cassidy's problems in his own power instead of surrendering to others who can help. Have you ever tried to do everything in your own strength? What happened?

10. What Bible verse helps you hold on when it seems the world around you is falling apart?

11. The theme of *Freefall* is 1 Corinthians 13:6-7 (NIV)—"Love does not delight in evil but rejoices with the truth. It always protects, always

trusts, always hopes, always perseveres." How does this verse relate to Shane and Cassidy's story?

12. Circumstances in our lives can change who we are. Cassidy lost faith and grew overly independent in the face of loss. Shane allowed his career to shape his behavior, making choices he never thought he was capable of making. Have you ever found yourself "different" in different situations? How can we stay true to who we are, even as circumstances change around us?

13. Have you ever been falsely accused of something? What happened and how did you deal with it?

14. How do you remind yourself that God is there when all of the circumstances around you seem to be against you?

15. If you were giving Shane and Cassidy advice on their wedding day, what would it be?

LARGER-PRINT BOOKS!

GET 2 FREE LARGER-PRINT NOVELS PLUS 2 FREE MYSTERY GIFTS

Love Inspired®
SUSPENSE
RIVETING INSPIRATIONAL ROMANCE

Larger-print novels are now available...

YES! Please send me 2 FREE LARGER-PRINT Love Inspired® Suspense novels and my 2 FREE mystery gifts (gifts are worth about $10). After receiving them, if I don't wish to receive any more books, I can return the shipping statement marked "cancel." If I don't cancel, I will receive 4 brand-new novels every month and be billed just $4.99 per book in the U.S. or $5.49 per book in Canada. That's a savings of at least 23% off the cover price. It's quite a bargain! Shipping and handling is just 50¢ per book in the U.S. and 75¢ per book in Canada.* I understand that accepting the 2 free books and gifts places me under no obligation to buy anything. I can always return a shipment and cancel at any time. Even if I never buy another book, the two free books and gifts are mine to keep forever.

110/310 IDN FVX5

Name	(PLEASE PRINT)

Address	Apt. #

City	State/Prov.	Zip/Postal Code

Signature (if under 18, a parent or guardian must sign)

Mail to the **Reader Service:**
IN U.S.A.: P.O. Box 1867, Buffalo, NY 14240-1867
IN CANADA: P.O. Box 609, Fort Erie, Ontario L2A 5X3

**Are you a current subscriber to Love Inspired Suspense books and want to receive the larger-print edition?
Call 1-800-873-8635 or visit www.ReaderService.com.**

* Terms and prices subject to change without notice. Prices do not include applicable taxes. Sales tax applicable in N.Y. Canadian residents will be charged applicable taxes. Offer not valid in Quebec. This offer is limited to one order per household. Not valid for current subscribers to Love Inspired Suspense larger print books. All orders subject to credit approval. Credit or debit balances in a customer's account(s) may be offset by any other outstanding balance owed by or to the customer. Please allow 4 to 6 weeks for delivery. Offer available while quantities last.

Your Privacy—The Reader Service is committed to protecting your privacy. Our Privacy Policy is available online at www.ReaderService.com or upon request from the Reader Service.

We make a portion of our mailing list available to reputable third parties that offer products we believe may interest you. If you prefer that we not exchange your name with third parties, or if you wish to clarify or modify your communication preferences, please visit us at www.ReaderService.com/consumerchoice or write to us at Reader Service Preference Service, P.O. Box 9062, Buffalo, NY 14269. Include your complete name and address.

LARGER-PRINT BOOKS!

**GET 2 FREE
LARGER-PRINT NOVELS
PLUS 2 FREE
MYSTERY GIFTS**

Love Inspired

Larger-print novels are now available...

LILP11B

FAMOUS FAMILIES

YES! Please send me the *Famous Families* collection featuring the Fortunes, the Bravos, the McCabes and the Cavanaughs. This collection will begin with 3 FREE BOOKS and 2 FREE GIFTS in my very first shipment— and more valuable free gifts will follow! My books will arrive in 8 monthly shipments until I have the entire 51-book *Famous Families* collection. I will receive 2-3 free books in each shipment and I will pay just $4.49 U.S./$5.39 CDN for each of the other 4 books in each shipment, plus $2.99 for shipping and handling.* If I decide to keep the entire collection, I'll only have paid for 32 books because 19 books are free. I understand that accepting the 3 free books and gifts places me under no obligation to buy anything. I can always return a shipment and cancel at any time. My free books and gifts are mine to keep no matter what I decide.

268 HCN 0387   468 HCN 0387

Name	(PLEASE PRINT)	
Address		Apt. #
City	State/Prov.	Zip/Postal Code

Signature (if under 18, a parent or guardian must sign)

Mail to the **Reader Service:**
IN U.S.A.: P.O. Box 1867, Buffalo, NY 14240-1867
IN CANADA: P.O. Box 609, Fort Erie, Ontario L2A 5X3

* Terms and prices subject to change without notice. Prices do not include applicable taxes. Sales tax applicable in N.Y. Canadian residents will be charged applicable taxes. This offer is limited to one order per household. All orders subject to approval. Credit or debit balances in a customer's account(s) may be offset by any other outstanding balance owed by or to the customer. Please allow 4 to 6 weeks for delivery. Offer available while quantities last. Offer not available to Quebec residents.

Your Privacy— The Reader Service is committed to protecting your privacy. Our Privacy Policy is available online at www.ReaderService.com or upon request from the Reader Service.
We make a portion of our mailing list available to reputable third parties that offer products we believe may interest you. If you prefer that we not exchange your name with third parties, or if you wish to clarify or modify your communication preferences, please visit us at www.ReaderService.com/consumerschoice or write to us at Reader Service Preference Service, P.O. Box 9062, Buffalo, NY 14269. Include your complete name and address.

FFBPA12